Also by Helene Lerner-Robbins:

Embrace Change
Finding Balance
My Timing Is Always Right
Stress Breakers

OUR POWER
AS
WOMEN

OUR POWER

AS
WOMEN

The Wisdom and Strategies of Highly Successful Women

Helene Lerner-Robbins

CONARI PRESS
Berkeley, California

Conari Press books are distributed by Publishers Group West.

Cover design: Ross Carron

ISBN: 0-943233-91-7

NOTE: Some of the names in the essays written by the author have been changed; others are used with permission. These stories also include some examples that are composites from people who have had similar experiences. In the last case, any resemblance to specific people or situations is coincidental.

CONARI PRESS

Library of Congress Cataloging-in-Publication Data
Lerner-Robbins, Helene, 1946–
    Our power as women: the wisdom and strategies of hignly successful women
/ Helene Lerner-Robbins.
        p.   cm.
    ISBN 0-943233-91-7
    1. Women—Psychology.   2. Success—Psychological aspects.   3. Control
    (Psychology)   4. Work and family.   5. Sex role.   I. Title
HQ1206.L448   1996
158.1'082—dc20   95-49453

This book is dedicated to Sarasvati, the goddess of learning and personification of all knowledge—arts, sciences, crafts, and skills.

contents

foreword

As a member of Congress, every day I have the opportunity to work together with my female colleagues to advance issues of importance to women. Every day, I see what can happen when women use their power to focus on the interests of other women, their families, and society as a whole. In other words, every day I see in practice the very phenomenon that Helene Lerner-Robbins discusses in this book.

I believe that it is important for women to exercise our power—not only to succeed as individuals, but in order to expand that power beyond ourselves to help other women. In my experience, women in elected office are more likely to offer legislation that benefits women and their families. I know this is true for women in other professions as well: Women advocate on behalf of the needs of other women. And when women exercise their individual power, there is a ripple effect that helps us all.

When I first came to Congress, a shocking study was released that disclosed the inequities in the treatment of women's health issues by the National Institute of Health (NIH). Working together, women members of Congress, women health advocates, and women's rights activists forced the NIH to change and improve its policies toward women. In addition, because of our efforts, domestic violence has finally been recognized for what it is—a violent crime. We were able to completely change the way domestic violence was viewed and treated by leaders in politics, law enforcement, the medical field and social service agencies and together we achieved a legislative milestone: the Violence Against Women Act.

These legislative successes in women's health and domestic violence programs show us how our world can be transformed and improved when women use their power to address problems women have faced for generations. And, just as my female colleagues and I work together in Congress, every day women work together in the business world, in their communities, and in their personal lives to create a better world for women and the rest of society.

When women stretch to reach new levels of success in both our personal and professional lives, we are able to achieve important and wonderful things. I urge all of you to read this book. When you are finished, you will feel ready to do just about anything—become active in your child's school, write a novel, start a clothing drive for the local shelter, or even run for office. And remember, when we work together, we can move the world.

Congresswoman Nita M. Lowey
Eighteenth District, New York
December 1995

Power—We Were Born With It!

This is a powerfully significant time for women. Even though we are in the workplace in greater numbers and this trend will continue into the twenty-first century, as individuals and as a group, we need to continue to exercise our power and learn new strategies to effectively overcome the obstacles in our path.

I know this from personal experience and from talking with many women. I had been working for other people most of my adult life, carving out a career in marketing and sales. Unfortunately, I was not pursuing my heart's desire—working with women to actualize their potential. Like many women, I felt a conflict between taking home a large paycheck ("the golden handcuffs syndrome") and doing what I really wanted to do. On weekends and at night, I managed to write books on stress and weight loss. In addition, I became a columnist for a well-known woman's magazine as an avocation, but I wanted to do more.

Then I had a child in my early forties and had to make a choice whether to go back to the corporation where I had been working prior to my pregnancy or pursue my heart's desire. My fear of the unknown drove me to tell my boss that I would come back. But the day before I was scheduled to return to work again, I realized I had been counseling women to face their fears and move forward in their lives; however, I was not able to take my own advice. So, after much reflection, I took a leap of faith and called the company late that afternoon to resign.

That moment was a turning point for me. I chose to follow my passion, to face the unknown, and not let my fear—which was enormous—paralyze me. On the whole, it has been a great decision. As an entrepreneur, I host and produce a television program on empowerment and wellness issues for women, as well as facilitate corporate seminars on mentoring, power networking, and career planning.

It hasn't always been easy juggling career and family responsibilities and being on the front lines. But the pluses of pursuing my vision far outweigh the minuses. One benefit is that the women I meet affirm that we can support each other to break through the obstacles that keep us from realizing our power— both externally and internally.

The main challenges for women of the '90s, as we approach

the twenty-first century, are to come from our strengths and use our power to structure new solutions for the ever-changing workplace. Simultaneously, we are striving to create successful personal relationships. In order to be effective in both areas, we must continue to seek a balance between home and career responsibilities. Not an easy task! But together we can share useful strategies that propel us forward. And that's what Our Power as Women means.

This book is a collection of my essays combined with excerpts from essays and interviews with other women about women and power: women's unique relationship to power, the obstacles to exercising our power, and how we can fully realize the resources within us. It is designed to inspire you as well as offer practical suggestions from women who have pioneered the way for us.

I care deeply about these issues and have given a great deal of thought to them. Over the past four years I've worked with hundreds of women as a consultant to corporate women's groups across the country. Their insights and stories appear throughout this book. Most of my essays on power are personal and pragmatic. For a look at political, economic, psychological, and spiritual perspectives on power, I've interviewed inspiring role models such as Gloria Steinem, Liz Claiborne, Patricia Ireland, Paula Zahn, Ronnie Gilbert (playwright, singer), Mary Jane Langrall (Director of Hospital Volunteers), and Adele Scheele (career coach). Finally, Geraldine Ferraro, Barbara Bush, Maya Angelou,

Beverly Sills, Ann Richards, Olympia Dukakis, Helen Caldicott, Sheila Widnall, Nita Lowey, Barbara Kennelly, Madeleine Kunin, Evelyn Fox Keller, Marianne Williamson, Sheila Wellington, Andrea Zintz (vice president of human resources, Ortho Biotech), and Mary Parish (consultant, author) have graciously allowed me to reprint their material about women's power. It is my heartfelt desire that our combined voices will encourage you to become the powerful and successful women that you have the potential to be.

The first section, *Women and Power,* defines power overall. By understanding all facets of our power, we can more fully express it. The second section, *Power Breakdowns,* presents the internal and external obstacles to our power as women, from the difficulties of juggling career and family responsibilities to the challenges of creating a successful career track—letting go of perfectionism and being able to give and get honest feedback.

The third section, *Power Build-Ups,* is devoted to how we can expand our power. We have a unique power that not only can be used to nurture our loved ones, but also can be used to build and lead teams in stressful work environments. We need to let others know our talents, abilities, and accomplishments, as well as powerfully communicate our ideas. We must chart long range visions for our personal and professional growth.

The fourth section, *Power Expanders,* is about how we can expand our power beyond ourselves to achieve our goals and those of others—to build coalitions with other women both at home and in the workplace. To practice love and forgiveness in our relationships so that we can achieve greater success in all areas of our lives, never forgetting that we access power by reaching out to others for help.

We as women have more options available to us than ever before. But if we are to continue to gain momentum, it is imperative that we find new ways of joining together in the workplace. Pioneering women are realizing the need to form groups based on career advancement and business issues. For example, today there are about one hundred corporate women's groups across the country using strategies that are inclusive of the men around them. Their example suggests that if we are to actualize our power, we must team with both our female and male colleagues.

I suggest that you read this book from cover to cover and keep it handy. When you are going through a particular challenge, reread the appropriate essay and draw upon the experiences of these women to develop creative solutions and derive inspiration. Together we can do what we cannot do alone. We can change our lives—and the world.

women
and
power

the facets of power

As we uncover and discover the political, economic, social, personal, and career facets of power, we gain new ways to use them. Just like diamonds grab the light and refract it into the many colors of the rainbow because of their facets, we can capture the full potential of our individual and collective power. The facets reflect our truly phenomenal nature as women.

"Let's dare to be ourselves, for we do that better than anyone else can."

—Shirley Briggs

Definitions of Power

I think the best way to start our exploration of power is to define it. If we look up the word in Webster's New Collegiate Dictionary, we find that one of its definitions is:

power: possession of control, authority, or influence over others.

More precisely, each of the component parts is defined as follows:

control: power or authority to guide or manage;

authority: power to influence or command thought, opinion, or behavior;

influence: the act or power of producing an effect without apparent exertion of force or direct exercise of command.

Power, in this definition, is described in relationship to others. So, power denotes that one has influence over others, guiding or managing others with authority, without the use of force. Power is also quite commonly thought to mean power over a process, i.e., manufacturing products or creating art. It can also be self-mastery, or the "ability to act or produce an effect," or "a source or means of supplying energy."

But is this how you define power? What is your experience of it in your everyday life?

I asked a number of participants in my seminars to define power. Here are some of their responses:

· *The ability to think clearly, work out ideas and make decisions;*
· *Making things happen, getting over our fears, changing negative thoughts to positive ones;*
· *The ability to get things done, taking control, influencing events, and getting people to do things the way you want them to;*
· *Winning the respect of employees, colleagues, and friends through knowledge;*
· *The ability to bring disparate things together;*
· *Taking charge of your life and claiming a direction for yourself;*
· *The ability to have a vision and carry it out;*
· *The ability to have control over our own situation—our own lives.*

From these definitions, I define power to be an active force that unifies, rather than destroys. It allows us to create our visions, be successful, and influence events and people. To be positive and have mastery in our lives. Is this what power means to you? Allow your definition of power to expand as you receive awareness from reading this book.

"It is a time of extraordinary challenge and change for American Society."

—Sheila W. Wellington

Power: A Historical Perspective

SHEILA W. WELLINGTON, *president of Catalyst, a non-profit research organization working to advance women in business*

The end of the twentieth century finds a woman up on a telephone pole or down in a Navy submarine, running a company or driving a big rig cross country. Women still serve coffee—but we also serve in the President's Cabinet. Nearly 350 female presidents run U.S. colleges and universities. Eight women hold Senate seats, and forty-seven women currently sit in the House. . . .

When I was a child, my mother told me the story of the fire at the Triangle Shirtwaist Factory. It happened in 1911 in New

York City, in the immigrant neighborhood where she grew up. A fire broke out in a factory where young women toiled in unimaginable conditions. Trapped in flames, 146 women died, piled against doors sealed tight to prevent their leaving before the day's work was over. The image—of all those women bolted into their jobs so they couldn't save themselves—seared into my imagination.

Many factors have led to the improved status of women, but the single most important was a national event that is now so taken for granted that few of us recognize its newness and its potency. Seventy-five years ago, on August 26, 1920, with Tennessee's ratification of the 19th Amendment, women gained the right to vote.

Women couldn't vote when my mother was born. Every time I think about it, it startles me. Even as Edith Wharton wrote her novels, as Helen Keller graduated from Radcliffe with honors, even as women manufactured the arms that led to victory in World War I and the nation's move to global primacy, women still could not vote. To make the ballot a reality, women and men of vision and guts, with many different goals and aims and views, came together. Recognized as having ideas, women would become individuals, would enter true adulthood.

Progress continues.

For thousands of years of human evolution, the critical factor distinguishing men's from women's work was physical strength. Men slaughtered the beast and dragged it home. Now, in the Information Age, what predominates is what Peter Drucker calls "knowledge work." Knowledge and ideas are the great equalizers. In intellectual labor, women can compete as equals. Women's brains go to work. And the smartest, ablest, most foresighted of both genders know this. . . .

We no longer see women literally locked into their workplaces. But we do find women struggling in outmoded workplace structures to balance their personal, family, and work lives. We find women struggling to have their voices, their ideas heard in the ranks of senior management and in the boardroom. There is still work to be done. . . .

Women have always worked, in the home or out of it. We always will. As the century closes, more and more women work for a pay check, while others find their own ways to contribute to society. But whatever American women do as the millennium draws to a close, we do it recognizing ourselves, and being recognized, as rational beings, as free citizens. This is the challenge of change the 20th century has wrought.

—*excerpt from Catalyst Awards Dinner*

> "If we think of ourselves as circles, our goal is completion—not defeating others. Progress lies in the direction we haven't been."
>
> —Gloria Steinem

A Community of Women

GLORIA STEINEM, *founder of* Ms. *magazine*

[Women's empowerment is] power over our own lives. I would say that empowerment goes a little deeper and encourages us to develop the unique self within us, to understand there is within each human being a true self that could never have happened before and could never happen again. It is a unique combination of heredity and environment over millennia that is essentially already there when we're born. It develops in many ways, but the voice within us is as important as the influences outside—not more important, but not less important either. We may call it a true self. We may call it a soul. We may call it a spirit. But I do think that spirituality is frequently the opposite of religion. Religion is usually a structure on the outside that tells you what to do. Spirituality is an inner guide.

The greatest impediments to power for women, of course, are patriarchy and racism. Those are the very deepest structures, and the beginning of hierarchy—the idea that men are supposed to dictate to women and that one race is supposed to dictate to another. Since they're based on differences at birth that can't be changed, and since they've been around from five to eight thousand years, they go very deep. We should consider that 95 percent of human history was pre-patriarchal. Perhaps we should just declare the last 5 percent an experiment that failed. The problem is that we read only about that 5 percent of history at the most. We only go back usually a few centuries or at most a couple thousand years because patriarchal scholarship declares the rest to be pre-history. I think that's a political label. It is a way of keeping us from knowing what existed for 95 percent of the time humans have been on earth.

There are no immutable or consistent differences between men and women. We're all human beings. The differences between two women or between two men are greater than those between males and females as groups. But cultural differences go very deep. I remember a group called something like the California Institute of Gender Identity that was trying to help teenage boys and girls who had been raised as members of the opposite gender—which happens for reasons of physical anomaly or family craziness. Chromosomally female teenagers had been raised as males—and vice versa. At the end of the study, the conclusion was that it would be easier to surgically change the sex of the teenager than it would be to change the conditioning they had incorporated by that time. That's how deep conditioning goes. Aside from reproductive capacity— if we choose to reproduce—it is society that creates gender.

The problem is not men, but the division of human nature into "masculine" and "feminine." If you look at the few cultures in the world where there is no institutionalized warfare or violence, their only shared characteristic is that the gender roles are not polarized. Girls are not taught to be submissive and passive in order to be "feminine." Boys are not taught to be assertive, controlling, even violent, in order to be "masculine."

The enemy of both men and women is gender roles. They're killing men eight years earlier than women. To change them, we need to raise boys more like girls. We've started to raise girls more like boys, but we need to do the reverse too. Because the so-called "feminine" qualities are only those qualities that are encouraged in females in order to raise children—empathy, flexibility, compassion, patience, and all those things. Men need to develop those too, just as women need to develop daring, assertiveness, and the human qualities called "masculine." It is about roles. Even now, some women are killers and some men are peacemakers. There is a big difference from one culture to the next. It isn't about being males or females, but the culture treats it that way, so it becomes true in the majority. The goal for all of us is wholeness. It's important to look at it that way because otherwise women will disdain "masculine" qualities and aggrandize "feminine" ones or vice versa. In either case, we won't develop the rest of ourselves.

In order to expand our power as women, first we need to imagine our power. The imagination of change is the first step toward change. Everything is a balance of opposites—for instance, the independent self and the communal self—so we need both faith in ourselves and in a community of women. I don't think we can do it alone, I've never seen that—even Helen Keller had a teacher. We all need somebody, at least one person, somebody who believes in us. Battered children and badly abused kids seem to have a chance of recovery as long as they have one person in their lives who sees what's happening to them, and says that it is wrong. Even if it doesn't stop, at least they begin to have faith that it's not their fault.

Everybody needs some community; human beings are communal people. Women are the only oppressed group that doesn't have a country—which is good, I think, because it makes us anti-nationalistic—but we don't even have a neighborhood. We don't even have a bar. That's why we need to make a psychic country with small support groups where we can try our best to speak the individual truth. Then we listen to others and see what the shared patterns are. That's helps us know that we're not crazy, the system is crazy. We can also share tactics. Some people use techniques like the ones I put in the back of *Revolution From Within;* for instance, imagining one's future self as a guide. So far, when I've talked to people about that, everybody imagines their best self, their true self, what they really want to be. It is important to remember that, if the possibilities of what you want weren't already real within you, you couldn't even dream them.

—personal interview

"One is not born a woman, one becomes one."
—Simone de Beauvoir

Women's Power Is . . .

Women's strength comes from our ability to be forceful, truthful, and compassionate. I used to be afraid that I would get stepped on if I exposed my warmth and showed my vulnerable side. Sometimes this has happened, and I've learned to discriminate whom I can and cannot trust. I now realize that those people who can't accept me are also most likely to be unable to accept themselves. Overall, the ability to give myself fully has been greatly rewarded both on the job and in my personal life.

When we use our power, we communicate confidently. And we inspire others because we are honest and exhibit integrity. More specifically, let's look at when we act powerfully and when we do not.

Power

When we. . .
Are able to understand what's
needed in a given situation and
take appropriate actions.

Take into account the needs
of other people, while taking
good care of our own.

Are direct and assertive in
communicating with others.

Have visions and create
our reality.

Team with others to solve
common challenges.

Dare to take risks
because we know that's how
change happens.

Practice patience. Knowing that
mastery is an incremental
process.

Loss of Power

When we. . .
React out of stress
and regret our actions.

Don't consider our own
needs a priority.

Are unable to communicate
our needs and resent
others who don't take
care of us.

Are confused and
look to others to
direct our thinking.

Are perfectionists and
do it all ourselves.
Don't delegate
or trust others.

Play it safe and rarely
attempt to do
things differently.

Feel frustrated when
we can't make change happen
right away.

> *"Our power lies in claiming it, and acting accordingly."*
> —Helene Lerner-Robbins

Take Power for Yourself

PATRICIA IRELAND, *president of the National Organization for Women*

I do a lot of college campus speaking and place a lot of emphasis on saying to these young women: think of yourselves as leaders. Think of yourselves as people with power to make change! They often don't think of themselves that way. Young men somehow assume they have a right to lead, and young women have to be convinced to go for it. . . .

I also find a greater understanding among young women, quite different, I think, than when I was young, of the fact that our lives are long and that there are different stages in our lives. And I've talked to a lot of these young women who are having families now, having them with the idea that yes, I may slow down my ascension in terms of the external world, I may start my political career in my thirties, instead of my twenties. But somehow they are taking it into account that they are going to live a long time. I think that I looked at it initially as I had to make a decision [career versus family], and that was pretty much it. I couldn't imagine how long life was. . . .

I am a tremendous believer in collective action. . . . Our ability to recognize that we have potential power and to act collectively to make change, that's one way to expand our power. I think the other real important shift that we've been advocating and seeing played out for a decade or more is to stop seeking derivative power. And that goes along with a different context. I think of it in the political context again because that's my business now—to stop begging the men in power for our rights and start taking power ourselves.

—personal interview

> *"The material manifestation of success is freedom.*
> *Freedom is power as well as happiness."*
> —Elizabeth Phillips, rare book dealer

Women's Economic Power

There are more women in the workforce than ever before. According to the U.S. Department of Labor Women's Bureau's May 1995 publication *Facts on Working Women*, women increasingly comprise a greater share of the total labor force. Here are some facts that will interest you:

· Women accounted for 46 percent of total United States labor force participants in 1994 and are projected to comprise 48 percent by the year 2005.

· Women's 1994 median weekly earnings 76.4 percent of men's. Even in traditionally female occupations, where women outnumber men, women still earn less than men.

In our society, which has been historically male-dominated, we face gender biases every day regarding economic power. In light of the many obstacles we face, how can we keep focused and empower ourselves in this area? Some ways include lobbying with other women for change and joining women's associations and corporate women's groups. There's power in women banding together and strategizing. What we cannot do alone, we can accomplish together.

There are some positive trends that are encouraging and helping businesswomen move towards equality:

- Women are becoming a "business imperative." Among others, Felice Schwartz, former president of Catalyst, has brought attention to the fact that women are now an important part of the talent pool in all types of industries.

- Corporate executives are increasingly recognizing there's a bottom-line benefit to a diverse workforce. The Civil Rights Act of 1991, formed the Glass Ceiling Commission with the mandate to study the barriers that keep women and minorities from the executive suite. According to the U.S. Department of Labor Women's Bureau: "Women have made substantial progress in obtaining jobs in the managerial and professional specialties. In 1984 they held one-third (33.6 percent) of managerial and executive and nearly half (48.5 percent) of the professional occupations. By 1994 they held 48.1 percent of managerial/executive positions and accounted for over half (52.8 percent) of workers employed in professional occupations."

· Employers are collaborating with women through professional organizations and corporate women's groups to bring about change.

Yes, progress is being made, but it will take a lot more work and carefully planned strategies to move through the barriers that constitute the "glass ceiling" for women. So, I encourage you to join women's networking/lobbying groups, stay focused on career mobility and request job performance feedback to help you advance in your profession.

> *"Women seem to have an interesting ability to bring disparate things together."*
>
> —Ronnie Gilbert

Exercising Political Power

NITA M. LOWEY, *congresswoman*

When I came to Congress in 1989, only 13 percent of the National Institutes of Health's budget was allocated for women's health needs. There were only three gynecologists on the entire staff of the NIH, our nation's premier research institution. Clinical trials systematically excluded female subjects. Believe it or not, even the lab rats were exclusively male.

And so the women in Congress demanded and secured a substantial increase in the attention and funding directed to our long-ignored health concerns. Today, there is a statutorily mandated Office of Women's Health. Last year, we increased funding for breast cancer research a full 40 percent. And now, by law, women must be included in NIH-supported clinical trials. It's not that our male colleagues opposed these changes; most just never thought to initiate them.

When the administration was formulating its health care reform proposal, the women's caucus insisted upon inclusion of expanded mammography coverage, and of the full range of reproductive services, including abortion. We led the fight [against]—and finally overturned—a congressional ban on Medicaid abortions for victims of rape or incest.

Women knew in a very personal way the difficult choices forced upon working parents, and fought for passage of the Family and Medical Leave Act. As a result, working women will not lose their jobs when they have children or need to care for a sick family member. . . .

On many other issues, women voted overwhelmingly for dramatic changes in government policy, often providing the margin of victory. . . . When we fight these battles, we aren't fixated on abstractions—success or failure are measured in flesh and blood. They make a difference for real people.

We know these people because we see them every day, staring back from mirrors. There is Lynn Woolsey, congresswoman from California, who raised children while on welfare. There is Carrie Meek, granddaughter of slaves, who worked as a domestic. There is Marjorie Margolies Mezvinsky, who has adopted children from around the world, raising them as her own. All are remarkable portraits of the American experience.

And we don't have to plead with Congressmen to listen to our agenda; we are in positions of power, we're setting the agenda. There is Pat Schroeder remaking our military from the Armed Services Committee. There are four women, including myself, setting budget priorities on Appropriations. There is Dianne Feinstein leading the fight on crime from Judiciary. Each wielding influence and authority.

By coming to the table, we combine at last qualities long-divided—empathy and power.

The irony is that so many of the policies on which women are working aren't just women's issues at all, they're life's issues. Life is a woman's issue. It just required a more complete experience, a different experience, to make that clear.

Would these changes have occurred without the leadership of women? Would the Congress have been able to lift these stories from grey statistical columns into the vivid world of real life? We may never know. . . .

It is so often the sad failing of the powerful to neglect the needs of the powerless. To assume that the concerns of all people are just reflections of their own. Because we know what it's like to be out of power, I think in large measure, women elected officials escape that pitfall. We share our power. We listen, we prod to get at how policy decisions will impact real people. And we engage people in discussions that lead to solutions. That is a very direct benefit of the collaborative style that women are particularly effective at utilizing.

But most important, we connect personally to the issues because that's how we've always done it. That's how our graduate school—the school of life experience—trained us.

—excerpt from Mt. Holyoke College Commencement Address

> *"When we face our fears and let ourselves know our connection to the power that is in us and beyond us, we learn courage."*
>
> —Anne Wilson Schaef

Courage: The Ability to Overcome

MAYA ANGELOU, *poet, author, scholar*

It takes a phenomenal amount of courage to be a woman today. For around this world, your world, my world, there are conflicts, brutalities, humiliations, terrors, murders. You can almost take any Rand McNally map and close your eyes and just point, and you will find there are injustices, but in your country, particularly in your country, young women, you have, as the old folks say, your work cut out for you. For fascism is on the rise, and be assured of it, sexism, racism, ageism, every vulgarity against the human spirit is on the rise. And this is what you have inherited.

However, on the other hand, what you have first is your courage. You may lean against it, it will hold you up, you have that. And the joy of achievement, the ecstasy of achievement. It enlightens and lightens at the same time. It is a marvelous thing. Today, your joy begins, today your work begins. You are phenomenal. I believe that women are phenomenal. I know us to be.

There is a poem called "Phenomenal Woman." I wrote the poem for black women and white women and Asian and Hispanic women, Native American women. I wrote it for fat women, women who may have posed for the before pictures in Weight Watchers. It wrote it for anorexics. I wrote it for all of us, for women in kibbutzim, and burgher women, women on the pages and the front covers of *Vogue* and *Essence,* and *Ebony* magazine. For we are phenomenal.

Now, I know that men are phenomenal too, because I, like you, have been told that 98 percent of all the species which have lived on this little blob of spit and sand are now extinct. And I know nature afforded them balance, so, Gentlemen, I accept your phenomenal nature. But I will tell you this—you will have to write your own poem.

> *Now you understand*
> *Just why my head's not bowed.*
> *I don't shout or jump about*

Or have to talk real loud.
When you see me passing,
It ought to make you proud.
I say,
It's in the click of my heels,
The bend of my hair,
The palm of my hand,
The need for my care.
'Cause I'm a woman
Phenomenally.
Phenomenal woman,
That's me.

from "Phenomenal Woman"

It is upon you [women] to increase the virtue of courage—it is upon you. You will be challenged mightily, and you will fall many times. But it is important to remember that it may be necessary to encounter defeat, I don't know. But I do know that a diamond, one of the most precious elements in this planet, certainly one in many ways the hardest, is the result of extreme pressure and time. Under less pressure, it's crystal. Less pressure than that, it's coal, less than that, its fossilized leaves are just plain dirt.

You must encounter, confront, life. Life loves the liver of it, ladies. It is for you to increase your virtues. There is that in the human spirit which will not be gunned down even by death. There is no person here who is over one year old who hasn't slept with fear, or pain or loss or grief, or terror, and yet we have all arisen, have made whatever absolutions we were able to, or chose to, dressed, and said to other human beings, "Good morning. How are you? Fine, thanks."

Therein lies our chance toward nobleness—not nobility—but nobleness, the best of a human being is in that ability to overcome.

—*excerpt from Wellesley College Commencement Address*

"Through commitment and action, we effect much needed change"

—H.L.R.

Call to Action

HELEN CALDICOTT, *founder of Physicians for Social Responsibility*

In 1980 I started an organization called Women's Action for Nuclear Disarmament, thinking women would be easier to mobilize than men because women became so concerned when they heard discussions of nuclear war. With twenty thousand members, it became the most effective lobbying organization in Congress. And for the first time in the history of the nuclear age, Congress has actually been voting against nuclear weapons and delivery systems for the past three years. Eventually, Physicians for Social Responsibility and related national medical organizations that I founded in other countries won the Nobel Peace Prize in 1985. Participants in the activities of the United States peace organizations and 80 percent of the peace movement in the United States were composed of women.

And other international peace organizations laid the groundwork for Mikhail Gorbachev to proceed with his extraordinary peace efforts globally. Never let it be said that a woman practicing full time medicine, raising three children, and engaged in a marriage cannot lead revolutions to save the earth.

Never forget that as you live your lives. I believe that people can only be ultimately happy if they are engaged in achieving goals higher than themselves. Certainly, salvation of the planet is not a bad place to start. And remember that 53 percent of the earth's population are women. Women do two-thirds of the world's work for which we earn 10 percent of the income; we own only 1 percent of the property; we have all the babies. And we have no power. This situation absolutely must change. . . .

The world is spending one trillion dollars a year on weapons of mass destruction. If you spent a million dollars a day since Jesus was born, you still would not have spent a trillion dollars. That trillion dollars, transferred from death to life, within ten years—the time we've got to save the earth from global pollution, overpopulation, species extinction, and the threat of nuclear war—would save the forty thousand children dying every day of starvation, would save the two-thirds of the world's children who are malnourished, would produce birth control and educate the women of the world so they stopped having massive numbers of children, would feed and clothe and house the children of the world and immunize them, would stop the forests from being chopped down, would plant billions of trees to save the atmosphere, preventing ozone destruction. It would stop the greenhouse effect, build mass transit systems, save this country, and save the world. The money is there globally; the technology is there to save the planet; the scientific and medical knowledge is there, but the political will is lacking.

It's time that you the people, but particularly the women, take your democracy into your hands and run your country, so that your country is run of the people, by the people, and for the children.

—*excerpt from Smith College Commencement Address, 1990*

power
breakdowns

fear & criticism

On the work front, many companies are being downsized to cut costs, reducing the number of employees. At the same time, both employers and employees are charged with creating greater efficiency—having to do more with less available resources. Of course, this creates increasing on-the-job stress, which most of us face on a daily basis. And with these pressures comes fear: Can I handle the added responsibilities? What if I fail? What if I lose my job?

Fear is a great impediment to power, for it causes us to recoil when we should forge ahead, become scattered when we should be more focused. When we're operating from fear, we cannot summon our rationality, intuition, or our ability to connect with other people. All of these are the cornerstones of our power as women.

Fear rears its ugly head in many forms, one of which is being overly critical and demanding of ourselves and others. This section will address our fears from a variety of perspectives.

"Being a recovering perfectionist, I have adopted as my motto the disclaimer often found on clothes made of raw silk: This garment is made from 100 percent natural fibers. Any irregularity or variation is not to be considered defective. Imperfections enhance the beauty of the fabric."

—Sue Patton Thoele

Let Go of Perfectionism

One factor that doesn't allow us to be powerful at work is perfectionism, because trying to be perfect stifles our creativity and our growth. Some of us may be perfectionistic about our performance stemming from standards others set for us, fearing that we may not be able to measure up to them. There are those of us who feel we have to be twice as good as our male counterparts to get ahead (and often this is true), and this pressure can create perfectionism.

However, living this way doesn't allow us to view making mistakes as a part of our growth process. And when we do make mistakes, which we are bound to, we may become defensive and retard our own advancement. For example, Carole, a financial analyst, got caught in her perfectionistic tendencies during a performance review at work. "My boss called me in and told me that she was basically pleased with my work and that I would be getting a pay increase. She then said that she would like me to make more decisions without consulting her. As she pointed this out, her positive comments took a back seat to her thoughts about how I needed to grow. I was feeling like I hadn't measured up to her expectations."

Carole needed to understand no one is expected to do a job perfectly. She needed to see that her boss was offering a valuable insight about how she could get ahead in the company—not criticizing her.

Our mistakes can be a great source of power if we learn from them and move on. Mastery of a new skill or achievement involves accepting that you will make mistakes. Margaret Maruschak, vice president of Bristol-Myers Squibb Company, knows this to be true. She told me over dinner, "In my thirties, I resolved to make new mistakes and not to repeat old ones." I like her attitude.

Being able to let go of perfectionism was empowering for me, too. When I started to write professionally, I struggled with putting my ideas on paper because I was trying to write "perfect" sentences. My creativity gushed when I took the advice of friends who suggested that I write down my thoughts without being concerned that my sentences were grammatically correct. I've learned to edit my material only after I've written down my initial thoughts. There is great power in just letting go and trusting that the right words will come to you. My perfectionist tendencies do return. Even now, when I give a colleague of mine a new manuscript to read for feedback, I have to breathe deeply and remind myself that her criticism will only make my work better. And when I hear her words, I've learned to be selective. I ask myself, do the suggestions fit? If they do, I reread the manuscript with them in mind. If they don't, I discard them.

Remember, letting go of perfectionism is part of a process of self-mastery. And as we begin to trust ourselves more, accepting our strengths and weaknesses, then we allow the best of ourselves to surface.

> *"Claiming our power involves putting the lessons of process into practice: not only learning from our mistakes, but giving and accepting feedback."*
>
> —H.L.R.

Learn to Give & Receive Honest Feedback

Why is it difficult for some of us to receive feedback? I think we have a hard time because we tend to take it personally, which doesn't allow us to evaluate valuable information that will help us grow.

One woman I know who understands the value of feedback shared with me, "A former male boss found it difficult to be honest with me. I think he thought I would break down and cry when I heard what he had to say. Of course, that's not true. I knew that if I didn't get him talking, I'd be stuck in the same job for years."

Feedback is invaluable, whether it's about your overall job performance or a project you're working on. It's one of the ways to improve your relationships with colleagues and bosses, and your chances of upward mobility in your company.

If you are not getting feedback from your boss, it's important to ask for it, i.e., "I'd like to set up a meeting next week with you to discuss my job performance, how's Tuesday at 3:00? If your boss avoids setting up a time, be persistent. Knowing how you are doing on the job is a priority for your advancing. It's one of the ways of finding out your chances for growth at your company.

An exercise that I and other experts have used that is helpful in processing feedback is: When someone offers you feedback, take a few deep breaths and concentrate on the sound of his or her voice as the feedback is stated. After she finishes, don't interject your point, but rather repeat to her what you have heard her say. By doing this, you'll gain some distance from what has been said which will prevent you from saying something that you might regret in the future. If need be, you can respond at another time, after you've had a chance to think calmly about what's been said.

Not only is it important that we be open to receiving feedback, but we must also be able to give it both in the workplace and in our personal lives. I don't want to be the type of friend or supervisor who feels one way and says something else. It takes courage to tell the truth. Some of us may fear that if we are honest, our friends or workers may not like it, and distance themselves from us. If this happens, then it's an indication that these relationships weren't on solid ground to begin with.

Graciousness is key when giving feedback. A supportive tone of voice, a direct and concerned glance, listening to any questions that may arise, and having compassion for how the person may feel about what you are saying are essential ingredients for good feedback techniques; enabling the information to be received by the other person in a open-minded manner.

"It is far more accurate and beneficial to tell ourselves that who we are is okay and what we are doing is good enough."

—Melody Beattie

Stretching or Pressing?

Many women today, myself included, have unusually high expectations of themselves and the people close to them. We are learning to stretch by challenging ourselves in every area of our lives—with family and friends, at the gym, and on the job. But stretching is very different than pressing ourselves. Stretching is an expansive state that leads to our taking positive actions. However, pressing suggests an unreasonableness, where we are asking too much of ourselves, demanding that we do better, grow more quickly, and too rapidly change our lives.

A colleague of mine, Edith, is an extreme example of a woman who pushes herself too hard. She never feels fulfilled by her accomplishments because she has her eye on the next challenge to tackle. Recently she has tried to be more nurturing with herself and says, "I find it difficult to rest and just enjoy myself. Recently, I hurt my back and had to stay in bed for a week. It was unbearable for me to lie in my bed with nothing to do. I thought about my life and how alone I feel despite my accomplishments. I'm afraid that if I don't try to change, I never will. I confided in a friend about how I felt and she responded, 'I've gone through those feelings too and am slowly changing my priorities. Over the past year, I've been asking myself, how do I want to shape my life in the next five years?' She told me about a few of her friends who get together for dinner each week to discuss these issues, and asked me to join them. I'm going to do it."

How can we take little steps towards not pushing ourselves too hard? By becoming aware of when we cross over the line, feel too tense, exhausted, or burned out. And when we are aware of this happening, we must change our direction: Do not work that extra hour or go to another engagement, but go out to dinner with a female friend (or take your husband and child out) or just go home; do the minimum of what has to be done, and go to bed early. Remember, no one is keeping score. Also, appreciate the special things that are in your life—a caring friend, lovely living quarters, a loving family. By bringing these things to mind, we nurture ourselves. We may even find that the need to press towards gaining another achievement diminishes.

"Acceptance of our fears heals the critic within."
                                              —H.L.R.

Quieting the Harsh Critic

Have you noticed what happens when our "harsh critic" (who lives in our heads) surfaces? It drains us of energy. Our focus is taken away from getting the job done and put onto disparaging ourselves or others—a sure way of depleting our power.

My friend Karen frustrated herself by being overly critical of a new employee. She says, "I had interviewed Max for the job and hired him based on several good references. The first three days at work, he didn't seem quite as sharp as I thought he would be. He wasted a lot of paper typing my letters several times. And I had to sit with him a good deal of the time to get proposals out. By the end of three days, I thought I had made a big mistake. He wasn't the self-starter I thought he'd be."

Karen's judgments of Max not only disempowered him, but also herself. Her fear of not being able to get the work out in a timely fashion led to her critical stance of Max, which destroyed both Karen's and Max's confidence and creativity. By criticizing him and not giving him the time to learn her company's way of doing things, Karen was taking away Max's chances to be successful. Furthermore, by having unrealistic expectations of her new employee and not taking the time to train him properly, Karen was not effectively using her power as a manager.

Left unchecked, our critical minds can latch onto anything—from what we don't like about a person's clothes to his or her hair color, posture, tone of voice. How can we train ourselves to be less critical, since for many of us, it's been a habitual response?

One way is to become more aware of how defeating it can be. This is made clear by looking at the difference between criticism and feedback. In the first case, you are probably angry or fearful and judgmental. People rarely want to hear criticism and will probably be turned off by it. In the latter case, your motivation for sharing information is to help the other person improve. Most people are willing to listen to feedback that is given in the proper spirit.

It's therefore important to catch yourself when you are being overly critical, whether with others or yourself. One way of changing this behavior is to turn your attention to something entirely different—read a report, help a co-worker, look at a beautiful painting in the office. As we become less critical, we may find that we will be more perceptive about how to handle situations that arise. In Karen's case, she may have been able to find a better way of working with her new employee.

> *"When we feel fear we shrink away, but when we're
> excited we go toward."*
>
> —Deena Metzger

Fear or Excitement?

Fears of succeeding or failing influence how we handle situations at work, even if we are not consciously aware of it. And it's possible that we have let our fears stop us from advancing to the next level, wavering between "I am capable of advancing?" to "can I really achieve it?" What helps to diminish our fears is the realization that we are all afraid at one time or another, even the person who owns and runs the company.

Lillian, a friend of mine, shared with me an incident that catapulted her growth. She says, "I was trapped in an elevator with ten other people a few years ago. It happened during my lunch hour and it took two hours for the rescue team to get to us. Most of the people with me were senior managers at my company, and I saw one of them become unraveled by this incident. At one point, the elevator shook and this man began to shriek, 'Get us out of here!' In the office, he always seemed so calm; I would have never thought him capable of behaving like that. The people who you think have it all together don't."

We need not let our fears stop us. In fact, many times when we think we are afraid, we may be excited. Our bodies react to fear and excitement in the same way (a quickened heart beat, perspiration, cold and clammy hands). I remember when I was promoted at my first corporate job, I was terrified about my new responsibilities and wasn't sure if I could handle the challenge. My mentor advised me that I wouldn't have been offered the position if others didn't think I could do it—and do it well. She also pointed out that positive changes are stressful and it sounded like I was more excited than afraid. Suddenly my attitude shifted. Her guidance and friendship gave me the permission I needed to feel excited about my new job. (I also knew that I could call on her for advice if I needed it.) Consequently, instead of being so frightened, I was looking forward to moving ahead.

You too can re-frame fear into excitement. New challenges are scary—and exhilarating. The next time you feel anxious about tackling a new task, remember that you have the skills or can acquire the necessary skills to meet the challenge.

"When fear motivates our actions, we diminish our power."

—H.L.R.

Coming from Strength

We are always evolving, and as we trust ourselves more, we will act from strength. This is no easy task and involves a process of learning to trust your instincts and logic, rather than reacting from a fearful place. There is a big difference between reacting to something and acting from strength. Reacting fearfully does double damage. We injure others but more importantly, we injure ourselves. Acting from strength, on the other hand is empowering. Here are a few examples of the differences between reacting from fear and acting from strength:

Reacting

You choose a course of
action based upon what
others think, going against
what you know will be
most useful.

You are unclear of how to
proceed in a given situation
and instead of waiting until
you understand what direction
to take, you act impulsively.

You cannot separate from
the stress of the moment.
Emotions rather than logic
guide your actions.

Acting from Strength

You are in a position of
authority and will not be
swayed by what others think.

You are aware that you
don't have sufficient
information to make a
decision. You let it be
known that a decision
will be made when that
information is received.

You are able to detach
from the apparent "crisis,"
and analyze the situation
before you act.

Practices to Strengthen Ourselves

· Meet or call a supportive friend sometime during the day.

· Read something inspiring and/or funny that puts things into perspective at the beginning or end of the day.

· At least twice a week, take a brisk walk sometime during the day to reduce stress, or do some other form of exercise.

· To bolster your confidence when making a difficult decision, think back to a past success when you were challenged and acted from strength.

· Build a network of people whom you respect and ask their counsel whenever you need it.

work & family conflicts

As we expand our skills and attain jobs of greater responsibility, we are faced with additional demands on our time. How do we both excel at work and manage to have a fulfilling family and personal life? This is one of the greatest challenges women face as we enter the twenty-first century. There are is plethora of issues that must be addressed, like child care and elder care, paid leave to care for newborns or ill relatives. To succeed, we must learn to let go of being "superwoman," and address the trade-offs for each decision on a daily basis. This section will focus on the juggling act from many different perspectives.

"Juggling 101 should be taught in colleges!"

—H.L.R.

A Juggling Act

PAULA ZAHN, *television anchor*

I think the biggest challenge women in America face today, particularly women who work outside the home, is striking a balance [between work and family], and we're working in a society that doesn't foster strong family values. I think in your heart you have to know what's right and, believe me, I think that in my industry people like Jane Pauley have been treated differently than people like Diane Sawyer and Connie Chung. Because for women with children in families, their lives are different.

I guess in my own world I have never felt compromised professionally because I'm married and because I have children. But I work very hard at that. I have been very careful not to turn down assignments when they in fact have very much complicated my personal life. I have a husband who is extremely supportive of what I do and I know what comes first. My family comes first. But there are times when I need to go on the road when in my heart I'd rather stay home. But I know I've got to do that.

You have to seek your own balancing act. Sometimes the scale falls too much in the work column and you fix it the next day. I know that I have no ambivalence about what my priorities are, because I know that, I think that I am able to strike a pretty good balance. Is every day perfect? No, absolutely not. . . .

I would say that behind every strong woman is a nice strong man. I think my husband Richard's support has been critical to my success. Richard has never viewed my success any differently than his own. He loves what he does. He also wants me to feel the same satisfaction. I know at times when I've been really tired and gotten a little down, he's been very good about prodding me along and saying, "that's natural what you're feeling, but it's important and you've got to do this."

I have very little personal time. I'll tell you what we have been doing lately that has worked out quite nicely. We make one date during the week and try not to break it. We started off saying "Okay this will be our time alone. We can't talk about the kids, the pediatrician, or the school assembly." Of course that never works. But the fact that we have an hour escape hatch, an hour a week outside the home, is very important. It's very liberating.

—personal interview

"My life is a juggling act. I've mastered keeping many balls in the air, while still maintaining a smile on my face."

—Stress reduction seminar participant

Balancing Career & Family

Learning to balance career and family responsibilities enables a woman to fully express her power. Unfortunately, most of us have a hard time doing that and, as a result, are under a great deal of stress. Between elder care (our responsibilities for taking care of aging parents) and child care (making sure that our children get the best of everything) every ounce of our energy and finances is parceled out. And there are trade-offs. Not all employers are sympathetic to our personal circumstances, and some may even demote us if we take time off to fulfill these obligations—creating even greater pressure on us. Although we want to advance and achieve our career potential, there is often a pull to be with our families to share more of the special moments, the struggles and the joys of our loved ones. And for those of us who have children, they grow up all too quickly.

Even if you don't voice these sentiments, chances are you feel them. Let's look at the following scenario: You come home to a four year old who says enthusiastically, "Mommy, let's play. I want to be with you." You are exhausted, hungry, and need time to unwind from a long, hard day, but you want to be with your child. So you play for awhile but are not fully attentive to him. Most of us have felt this way at one time or another, and have been frustrated by spending so many hours in a stressful work environment that we can't enjoy rolling around on the floor with a little one who is adoring.

I don't have any pat answers to the conflict between career and family because, like everyone else, I often feel pulled in several different directions. But I do know that I keep re-evaluating my priorities along the way, and if I find myself working too much and not spending quality time with my son, I will adjust my schedule. After all, he'll only be five once.

One of the things that makes this conflict a little easier is to get the best care for our children for the times when we can't be with them. For example, I screened more than 100 prospective sitters until I finally found the right person. The effort was worth it to find the right person to watch my son because now I can go to appointments with peace of mind. My requirement for good child care is someone with authority who is cheerful and willing to play his games—not just watch him play them.

I've also learned how important it is to have some quality time with my son each night (if I'm not traveling), even if it's for a short period—time when I make a conscious effort to be there as fully as I can for him, like having dinner together and finding out about his day, playing a game or reading him a story. It's our way of connecting. In our family, we also try to do something special at least one day during the weekend. And we take vacations. (They are a necessity.) If we don't take time out for fun together, we all suffer. I, for one, become testy and irritable and am not very pleasant to be around.

I also know the value of setting aside time for myself, by myself, such as a monthly massage, and a nightly luxurious ten-minute bath. These are my replenishment rituals. Whatever yours might be, remember to make them a part of your regular routine so that you'll be able to more calmly deal with the work/home conflict.

"Believe in a love that is being stored up for you like an inheritance, and have faith that in this love there is a strength and a blessing so large that you can travel as far as you wish without having to step outside it."

—Rainer Maria Rilke

Having It All

BEVERLY SILLS, *Chairman of the Board, Lincoln Center for the Performing Arts, Inc., and opera singer*

Women are told today that they can have it all. I would like to tell you that if the word "all" means career, marriage, and children, then you can have it, but someone is going to pay for it. This "all" can bring you every kind of fulfillment, excitement, fun, rewards, but you really have to make a total commitment to making it work. You will need lots of give, lots of compromise, lots of humor. You will have to be competitive, but only enough to be exciting and not, for God's sake, enough to be bored. You will need to be proud of your femininity, but you will have to substitute the words "our thing" for "my thing." And you will cry a lot, that is the career part.

And then you will have to take a close look at the child. In my house her name was Muffy. She didn't want me to be glamorous, she didn't want me to be humorous, she didn't want me to be supportive, she just wanted me around. She wanted me to love her, to be there when she needed me, and she needed somebody to depend on. Her mind was made up, so I couldn't confuse her with the facts of my life. She had to pay the price for my wanting it all. To delay in having a baby until you are "ready" can be very dangerous to your health and the baby. Not to have a baby at all could be a great loss to you, and to have a baby without a real commitment on your part could be a great tragedy.

So you can have it all, but there are two keys to this kingdom. The first is that you have to believe in yourself and you have to know that you can make it work. And the second is love. You're going to have to ooze it from every pore. You're going to have to love your work passionately—love it enough to feel it's worth the nightmare of days that are twenty-nine hours long. You're going to have to love your husband so that when he complains about your twenty-nine-hour day you will have the patience to soothe him, the desire to comfort him, and the ability to turn your twenty-nine-hour day into a thirty-hour day—the last hour for him alone. And you are going to have to love your child and not just hear its needs, but feel its needs, touch and hold and never let that child feel that anything is more important to you in the whole world. So what if the day is now thirty-one hours long. You can sleep in your old age if you live long enough to enjoy it. But I have to tell you that you owe it to yourself to try for it. You may be disappointed if you fail, but you are doomed if you don't give it a try.

A lot of us were meant to be spectators in life and that is okay, too, because an audience is just as important as a performing artist. But some of you who have the guts and desire to get into the middle of the arena and fight the bull in every sense of the word, I will tell you that I recommend it highly and I wish you the best of luck.

—excerpt from Smith College Commencement Address

"To be like a child and play like a child is the wisest thing one can do."

—H.L.R.

The Power of Play

Some of us don't take time out of our busy schedules to play. We may even feel that it's a waste of time. Unfortunately, we lose sight of our need to replenish ourselves. A woman's basic needs are not only food, clothing, and shelter, but also caring, friendship and FUN. Yes, fun works wonders. Fun lightens our burdens, gives us new perspectives, and frees our minds to face ordinary situations with renewed enthusiasm. Here's a case in point:

Did you ever come home from work feeling so tired that the only thing you were capable of doing was brushing your teeth and crawling into bed? Take this same scenario and add to it a phone call from your best friend, who loves to joke with you. You hear her laugh and your exhaustion goes away. Instead of wanting to go to sleep, you'd rather meet her and go dancing.

Playing is not just for little children. A few good jokes,

drinking a cappuccino with a special friend, roller-skating with your children, swimming, collecting shells on a beach—all of these activities can transform exhaustion into energy. We all have a child inside us that wants to have fun, but do we let her come out to play? You know what she'll do if you don't! Throw a tantrum in the form of being bored, exhausted or uncooperative.

I'm learning to put more play time in my life and am experiencing some of the benefits. For example, a few months ago I had to work three Saturdays in a row. I love what I do, so it wasn't that I didn't want to show up for work, it's just that I wanted to play as much as I wanted to work. On one of these Saturdays, I teamed up with a colleague who felt the way I did so we decided to make our business trip fun. After our meeting, we got on the train, kicked off our high heels, opened our suit jackets, and didn't talk one stitch of business. By the end of our ride, we were giddy. I guess we created a new type of "sandbox" for ourselves.

We need to find the balance between work and play in our lives. Let's face it, there is always something more for us to do either at home or at the office. The chores are endless. I've noticed that if I have the willingness to stop "working," the next right activity takes place. Sometimes it's just resting or sometimes it's laughing with a friend and telling jokes.

"When people keep telling you that you can't do a thing, you kind of like to try it."

—Margaret Chase Smith

Take Pride in Your Choices

GERALDINE A. FERRARO, *former candidate for Vice-President of the United States*

Today, in America, women can be whatever they want to be. We can walk in space, and help our children take their first steps on earth. We can run a corporation and work as wives and mothers. We can be doctors and we can bake cookies at home with our six-year-old future scientists.

Or we can choose none of these. We don't have to be superwomen. For the first fourteen years of my marriage, I worked at home as a mother and wife. That was a fine profession, and nothing I have done since has filled me with more pride and satisfaction. For me, it was the right thing. Then I decided to work outside the home, and that was also the right decision for me. Not every woman would agree with my decisions, but the point is, they were my own—I made them for myself. I know that every woman can take pride in whatever she chooses to do. . . .

Let me share a letter I received from a Rhode Island woman with two young daughters, aged four and two. "I brought my two girls to a rally for you in Providence, because I wanted them to see you. I wanted them to know what they could aspire to, that the possibilities for them were limitless, that they could, if they wanted, be President, and that being female would not preclude them from doing or being anything they chose."

That was really what our campaign was about—making America the best it can be by using the talents of every American. And that is why, whatever else happened in 1984, I will never regret the campaign. It was a gain, not just for women—it was a plus for all Americans. We took down the sign that said "Men Only" on the door of the White House. That was more than an idea for 1984—that was an ideal to carry us to the year 2000 and beyond. . . .

You are free to rise as far as your dreams will take you. Your task is to build the future of this country and of our world. You are our new global citizens. Whatever you do, I remind each of you that your potential and possibilities at this juncture of your lives are limitless.

—*excerpt from Wellesley College Commencement Address*

"Getting to our power is like exercising, each day we must make a commitment to focus ourselves and define who we are."

—Brenda Ginsberg

Stay Focused

One obstacle that gets in the way of our maintaining balance and attaining our goals is feeling overwhelmed by the many demands on our time, and not concentrating fully on what we are doing at the moment. Estelle, a senior manager, recently shared with me a technique that helps her stay focused. She says, "I think of myself at the center of a wheel. The spokes emanating from me represent my work, family, social, and community responsibilities. I play many roles in my life, and I've learned to focus my energies on one area at a time. For example, I head the local PTA. That part of me isn't in the foreground during my workday. Nor is the fact that I'm a mother uppermost on my mind when I'm dealing with how to strategize a new product launch. And I do this with peace of mind, because I've sought a lot of help along the way so that I know my children are well-taken care of when I'm not around. I rely on my baby-sitter (my mom), and my husband who helps out with some of the children's emergencies."

There are many techniques to keep us in the moment; ask your friends or colleagues to share with you the ones they use. A technique I like to use to keep my attention on the task at hand and not worry about something from another area of my life is to pause for a moment before I undertake an activity.

Try pausing now. Sit in a chair with your feet on the floor and take a few deep breaths. Bring to mind a supportive thought like, "Right now I am going to focus on finishing this project and I have plenty of time to do it. Later, I'll tackle the rest of my work. It will all get done." Now you are ready to start the activity.

"What distinguishes humans from animals is their ability to consciously decide that they have had enough!"
—H.L.R.

Selfish or Self-full?

One of the ways we disempower ourselves is to focus on others to the point of neglecting ourselves. Women have traditionally been nurturers, and it is natural for many of us to give, but the problem arises when we take this to the extreme—taking care of our families, bosses, and co-workers and not taking equal time to replenish ourselves. (Some of us even feel selfish when we take time out of our busy schedules to meet our own needs.)

Sheila knows the dilemma all too well: "I've been divorced for four years and my responsibilities seem endless. Last month, my job required that I travel through three states within three weeks, which meant that I gave up two of my weekends. Juggling between baby-sitters wasn't easy. I felt so stretched that the other day, I almost screamed at my boss when she asked me to take on an additional project. And I don't see things lightening up until next month." Sheila confessed that she needed some time with her family and some time to just relax by herself; however, she can't seem to get off the treadmill.

She is typical of some working women who are great doers, but the perpetual doing has a price—their serenity and well-being. A colleague of mine, Fran, became sick last year because she didn't take a vacation. She says, "I know that I need at least two vacations a year, but when December came around (a time when I usually take one), I didn't. Instead, I worked right through the holidays. I could feel myself getting sick, but I was driven to fulfill my responsibilities and couldn't take a break. I ended up with a high fever, pink eye, needing megadoses of vitamins and rest. Why couldn't I have rested sooner?"

Endless doing for others robs us of our power. In a culture that praises doers, many of us feel uncomfortable just resting and relaxing. Our power lies in our ability to give ourselves the care we would give other people. And, ironically, when we take care of ourselves in this way, the people around us also get our very best.

> "If the first woman God ever made was strong enough
> to turn the world upside down all alone, these women
> together ought to be able to turn it back, and get it right
> side up again! And now they is asking to do it, and
> men better let them."
>
> —Sojourner Truth

Agents of Change

MADELEINE M. KUNIN, *Deputy Secretary of Education, former
Governor of Vermont*

If women are to continue to enter fields traditionally occupied
by men in law, medicine, politics, science, education, is it
enough to simply be there, in roughly equal numbers with
men, or, is it time to change the values, the structure, the style
of these traditionally male institutions and begin to claim them
as our own? . . .

Expressed in terms of women and power, rather than simply exercising it, is it not our responsibility to exercise power
differently?

I believe that if we find a comfortable mode of integrating our female selves with the institutions and organizations we join, we will rise up the ladder to leadership positions and be able to change how these institutions function, making them more accommodating to women's lives as well as more appropriate to the values and needs of our time.

I believe we are entering a new period in our evolution towards full equality as women, a period when we will be able to "change the world," and rather than submerging the female experience to do so, we may celebrate it and learn to express ourselves, not only as indistinguishable equals, but speak in our own women's voices.

No longer would marriage, motherhood, and the general experience of being born female be viewed as draining and sidetracking subchapters of our goal-oriented lives.

No longer would women's lives be seen as a balancing act, or as one of sacrifice, all tilted towards one end of the scale or the other—family or work; love or power—women's lives would be integrated, just as men's lives have aspired to be. . . .

It's not too ambitious to think of changing the world if you think about it one step at a time: changing the way power is exercised in the corporation, the way power is exercised in Congress, in state houses, in city halls, and the way power is exercised in the hospital, the university, the laboratory.

Our challenge—at this stage of women's evolution—is to

enable women to integrate the cycle of our lives as women with the cycle of our lives as leaders, as agents of change.

Rather than accommodating to the world as you find it, charged with confidence in your competency and your values, and yes, in your womanhood, you can and must change the world to more closely approximate your ideal. . . .

—excerpt from Barnard Commencement Address

power
build-ups

role models
& mentors

Knowing that we are not alone in our personal and professional challenges, that women have pioneered the way before us, and will come after us, helps us tackle seemingly impossible tasks. In the media, at the office, in our community, women's achievements are becoming more visible than ever before. Here we look at role models and mentors from many points of view.

"Everything nourishes what is strong already."
—Jane Austen

Reflections from a Role Model

SHEILA E. WIDNALL, *Secretary of the Air Force*

A committed mentor who is an expert in a young person's chosen field can be a primary gatekeeper for the self-esteem of a [student], her rate of progress toward her goal, and career interests. In my experience, a mentor's high quality support and continual interaction can shape a student's goals, productivity, self-image, and chances of success. Let me clarify that men, as well as women and minorities, need mentors. We all need encouragement, and any institution needs the talents of the entire population. Mentors and role models who can identify with, attract, and retain people from all walks of life bolster the viability and health of their institution. Diversity helps keep an institution relevant. It boosts overall quality. It offers a face that looks like America. . . .

A few thoughts on my appointment as the first woman service secretary. I view it as an opportunity, not an achievement. It's also a substantial responsibility and great fun—no other job would have brought me to Washington. No other could be as exciting.

In the last few months, I've had the chance to fly in an F-15 over Alaska and in an F-16 over the test range at Edwards—a night mission, pitch black, 200 feet off the ground, 500 miles an hour, relying on a night vision system for navigation and targeting. An intense flight—and having me along for the ride must have turned up the heat for the pilot. But you'd never know it. The aircrews I've met are consummate professionals—just like the rest of the Air Force.

My acceptance by senior Air Force leadership has been truly extraordinary. I have been met with enthusiasm, trust, openness, collegiality, loyalty, and support. They want to approach the organization's great challenges as a team. And having spent time with Air Force people across the country and at all ranks, I'm very moved when they say, "We're glad you came to the Air Force. We're glad you came to our base. We want to share with you what we do and how we live. We want to stay on your wing."

People ask if I planned to be Secretary of the Air Force. For a long time I thought about it—but not since the age of four, as newspapers have reported. I'm not that good a planner.

But being the first female service secretary has turned out to be better than anything I could have possibly imagined. I'm thrilled the Air Force likes to be first!

—excerpt from "Women of Distinction" Awards Dinner

"The three ingredients for a mentoring relationship are providing support, challenging growth, and sharing visions."

—Andrea Zintz, vice president, human resources, Ortho Biotech, Inc.

Finding Mentors

In counseling working women, a common theme that arises is the need for mentors, women and men who can advance them in the workplace. The traditional mentoring relationship, as defined by some experts, involves a mentor (a more experienced person) and protegé (less experienced person). In this model, the mentor gives knowledge to a protegé, and the information flow is usually one-way. Unfortunately, as a result of the numbers of women entering the workforce today, there are not enough mentors for everyone. Also some women aren't comfortable with the traditional arrangement, which tends to be quite patriarchal in design. We must therefore look for alternatives.

I suggest to my clients that first they break down the various roles that a mentor plays, i.e., coach (gives you support and encouragement), confidante (listens to your challenges), counselor (guides you in the right direction), and sponsor (introduces you to the "right" people). Then build a mentoring network by asking a different person to fulfill each role. You're more likely to have busy people help you out if you ask one thing from each one of them. These relationships are mutually advantageous and involve continuity and commitment (usually, mentoring relationships last for awhile, as distinguished from networking contacts which need not). Today, I call you for feedback; tomorrow, you may be calling me to introduce you to my new boss. Also, mentors are not necessarily people at a higher level than you. Your pool of mentors can be taken from colleagues and employees at lower levels than you who have knowledge or skills that you want to learn.

To initiate your mentoring network, I suggest creating a prospect list. To do this, write down both women and men you've known from your current work situation, past jobs, community and professional associations. Even if you haven't talked to a person at great length, if he or she knows who you are, put them on your prospect list.

Don't delay in setting up initial meetings with one of your mentoring partners. You don't want to miss out on valuable time and information that can help you succeed. Brainstorm with a supportive friend about how you should make the initial contact, i.e., if you know that person comes in early and has coffee in the company cafeteria, perhaps that is an appropriate time to talk with him or her. Think about your approach carefully and plan this important first meeting.

During the meeting with a potential mentor, establish a common bond—bring up a similar interest, or acknowledge one of her projects that you're excited about. It is very important not to start by asking her to be your mentor. It's a turn off. You'll be sending out a message that she will have to do a lot of work. Instead, engage her in an opportunity that will support her growth, as well as yours. Let her know that you will share with her any information that can support her projects.

For example, Sarah wanted to create a mentoring partnership with a colleague, Ruth. The two women had been acquaintances, nothing more. Ruth failed to return several of Sarah's phone calls. Sarah was determined to establish this relationship and thought a lot about how she could win Ruth over. She knew Ruth would profit by being introduced to one of her clients, so after work one evening, she dropped into Ruth's office and said, "I've know just the person to advance your project." She gave Ruth the contact, and that was the start of a mutually beneficial relationship.

> *"Together, we can coach ourselves to Win!"*
>
> —H.L.R.

Female Coaches

PAULA ZAHN, *television anchor*

In my career, I only have had one person that I would truly call a mentor and that is Barbara Walters. I think the reason why so few people have taken an interest in my career is that we're all too busy climbing a ladder. I think that Barbara has had such enormous success that she can feel comfortable helping me along and she can have a generosity of spirit that other women can't. She's at a point in her career where she's not intimidated, certainly not by my success, and I have found it very comforting to lean on Barbara from time to time because it can be very lonely working the sphere that I'm working in. . . .

It's sort of interesting how [our relationship] happened. I had worked at ABC News for about two years when CBS News came knocking on my door. At that time I had only met Barbara socially. I'll never forget when CBS News came to me and said, "We want to hire you to do CBS This Morning, but you have to decide in the next twenty-four hours what you want to do." Now, of course, it had taken me eighteen years to figure out that I wanted to go to a network in the first place; I certainly was not going to be able to decide in twenty-four hours if I was going to change networks. And it set off a really interesting series of events.

The news spread through ABC like wild fire that I was contemplating leaving. I had an intense meeting with the heads of Capital Cities ABC. I'll never forget after having spent two and a half hours with the CEO who pleaded with me to stay, I got back to my office and on hold was Barbara Walters who had been waiting for me for several minutes. I picked up the phone and said, "Hi Barbara," and all she said was "Hi Paula, you have absolutely no choice, you must go to CBS."

We talked for quite a bit of time, and what was interesting about that one single call was that things were happening so quickly, I really didn't have a chance to think about the bigger picture. I was happy at ABC. They were going to give me some good opportunities, so there really didn't seem to be any reason to leave. But what Barbara said to me was "Paula, they're promising these things for you tomorrow, and CBS is today. There is no risk in taking this new job. The worst thing that can happen is you'll fail. But if that happens you certainly will be a lot better known by that time." Barbara's theory was really pretty valid. She basically said "this is your one shot at exceptional national exposure and even though you're happy at ABC, and I understand your ties to the organization, you have nothing to lose. Go try it." And in the end, you have to listen to that voice inside yourself that drives you but I will tell you that Barbara gave me the strength to cross the street.

—excerpt from a personal interview

> *"I am going to be like a warrior, I am going to fight and if I don't win, then at least I've tried."*
> —Paloma Cernuda, breast cancer victor

Women Warriors

We can learn a lot about power from women who have faced tragedy and transformed their lives despite it. I have been privileged to know some breast cancer victors who have re-evaluated their lives and their priorities as a result of having the disease. They are important role models for me. Let me share with you the insights that I have received from these courageous women. To seize power now. To make each moment count. To live fully. One woman told me that since her diagnosis, she lives each day as fully as she can, whereas before breast cancer she lived at about half of her capacity.

How often do we go around existing, rather than living? Thinking about what will happen next or what has passed, instead of living in the moment. Some breast cancer victors who have brushed with death know the value of the moment. They realize that all there really is—is this moment, NOW.

Susan Markisz, a breast cancer survivor, knows this to be true. She says, "I'm married and have two wonderful children. Since my diagnosis a few years ago, I have experienced a range of emotions that I never knew I had. I started to create self-portraits, really as an exercise to understand myself better. My photographs were full of anger, fear, and disbelief. In many of them I was covering up my mastectomy scar. The process of healing is a long one and I appreciate little things much more now, like laughing with my young daughter as we roll around on the floor together. Time is precious to me. Coming through this dark period has filled my life with new purpose. I want to show my work to other breast cancer survivors so that they can see their beauty and strength."

Other breast cancer survivors have also come to new awarenesses. For example, Addie says, "My teenage daughter was always challenging me, and I'd go for the bait. As a result of my experiences with breast cancer, I have realized that most things aren't worth fighting about. My daughter is going through a rebellious stage and that's what teenagers go through. I don't take it so personally anymore. Of course, I'm not perfect and slip back into fighting at times, but I'm restraining myself more than I used to. As a result, I have the energy to devote to working with other activists to find a cure for this dreaded disease."

Both Addie and Susan are role models. Their appreciation

for how precious their time is can help us realize what our true priorities are. It is not easy to give up an old habit that drains our power, like getting caught up in arguments about things that don't really matter. How can we begin to break this negative pattern? An effective tool for disengaging from an argument is to ask yourself the following questions before reacting: "How important is it to win this one? What price am I paying for being right?" In most cases, if not in all, it isn't worth the fight. Remember, the price we pay for winning petty victories is increased stress, which keeps us from accomplishing important goals.

> *"Nobody can make you feel inferior without your consent."*
>
> —Eleanor Roosevelt

Looking Behind the Packaging

EVELYN FOX KELLER, *Professor of History and Philosophy of Science, Massachusetts Institute of Technology*

It was feminist theory that taught me first to see, and ultimately to look behind the packaging, to think seriously about what this disparagement—of women, of their traditions, of their abilities, of their accomplishments—that had been so consistently a part of my own education had meant for me and for women in general, and even more, what it had meant for science.

What, for example, did people mean when they spoke of thinking scientifically as thinking "like a man?" Wasn't the central claim of science precisely to a methodology that transcends human particularity, that bears no imprint of individual or collective authorship? I have to confess that I did then, and in fact still do, think like a man: I was logical and, as they say, "tough-minded." But it wasn't exactly logic that led me to see the contradiction that was embedded in a tradition that equates objectivity with masculinity, or that led me to wonder about the kinds of thinking which, by this equation, were supposed not to belong in science just because they were thought of as "feminine." That led me, finally, to think about the kinds of thinking that, by this same equation, would have been called "thinking like a woman" had they been called thinking at all, even though practiced by men and women alike, and by our very best scientists at that. Rather than logic, what led me to examine those kinds of thinking that clearly were, and would have been even more, useful in science had they not been denigrated as "feminine," was the courage I had gathered from feminism. The courage to take seriously all those common-place associations that pervaded our informal thinking and speaking about science, yet barred from our formal thinking—to not only take this informal knowledge seriously, but to rethink the meaning of science through the lens that it provided. In a word, feminism empowered my very scientific need to know—both about things and about science itself, though perhaps in somewhat unconventional ways. It taught me to look behind the conventional discourse about science, and in the process, inspired me to look again at the heroic women that science had slighted.

Barbara McClintock was one of these. When I first began my study of McClintock's life and work, she was widely adored by her colleagues, but excused from full membership in the brotherhood of science by what was seen as her personal, professional, and even methodological eccentricity. Her revolutionary work on genetic transposition was regarded as perhaps true, but surely not of any great significance for biology. By 1983, all that had changed. Only five months after my book on McClintock was published, she was awarded the Nobel Prize, and, with that legitimation, became available as a model for scientists everywhere, women and men alike. Cecelia Payne Gaposchkin was another woman slighted by the conventional telling of scientific history, her full story remaining still to be written. . . .

The lessons we learn from these women's lives are not only of historical value; they empower us by their examples to persist in our own struggles, to assume the courage of our own convictions.

—*excerpt from Mt. Holyoke College Commencement Address*

"You need only look around you to see your passion in another woman's face."

—H.L.R.

The Power of Passion

Since the Women's Movement of the '60s, many of us have been able to eliminate what we don't want in our lives. More and more, we are not afraid to stand up for ourselves, stating our needs and getting them met by the appropriate people. We've become visible, able to go forward to achieve our visions and dreams.

Today's women are both committed and intelligent. It's exciting to be part of a group of individuals who are exploring their creativity and redefining what it means to be a woman. We are filled with passion, that vital force inside of us which longs to express itself. It is at the very core of our being. Our drive, intensity, quest for the truth—our desire to do and be our very best, not to stop until we achieve our goals, is inspiring.

This force is what attracts others to us and creates our aliveness.

Our passion is contagious and empowers other women whom we meet. I recently heard Dr. Susan Love speak to an auditorium of breast cancer survivors. She is smart, honest, and confrontational. To be in her presence made me feel affirmed as a woman. After leaving the presentation, I found that I was willing to press a little bit harder to reach one of my seemingly impossible goals. (Who says we don't have role models?)

Our peers can be our role models and we can be role models for other women. Every time one of us achieves success, we all profit. The fact that I overcome obstacles in my professional life can wake up another sister to the truth that she can do it too.

About a year ago, I attended The Women of Enterprise Awards, hosted by Avon Products Inc., where passion, courage, and perseverance were in abundance. Women entrepreneurs filled the grand ballroom of the Waldorf-Astoria to honor several women for their outstanding merits in business. These honorees had overcome many obstacles in their lives. In fact, they felt that their challenges had shaped them into the successes they are today.

Express your passion. It is the power within you that inspires change, generates movement, and propels others to action.

developing your skills & talents

We always have the potential to grow. What's needed to move forward is a willingness to hone our skills and talents, both professionally and personally, in order to increase our power and effectiveness in the world. That's why to make the investment in ourselves is one of the greatest gifts we can give to ourselves—and to others.

*"As vital as communication is, many of us have been
trained to do it in ways which alienate us from others
rather than connect us to them."*

—Sue Patton Thoele

Power Communication

Our words have an impact on ourselves and others. Therefore, it's not only important to think and speak positively, but
also to honor another person's style and use their style when
communicating to them. This makes people open and more
willing to listen to what you have to say.

Unfortunately, we may not acknowledge our differences.
Deborah Tannen addresses this point in her book *You Just Don't
Understand:* "We feel we know how the world is, and we look
to others to reinforce that conviction. When we see others acting as if the world were an entirely different place from the
one we inhabit, we are shaken. . . . Being able to understand
why this happens—*why* and *how* our partners and friends,
though like us in many ways, are not us, and different in other

ways—is a crucial step toward feeling that our feet are planted on firm ground."

It's important to become more aware of and have respect for how diverse our communication styles are. Experts have created models that categorize these differences and there are many books on the topic. It might be useful to read one of them.

Here's an example of how a woman in one of my seminars was able to reverse a difficult situation when she acknowledged the differences between her communication style and that of a co-worker. "We don't get along," complained Sharon. "I feel like we talk at each other, not to each other. It's very frustrating. There has to be a better way of working together." I suggested that she start by observing her co-worker in a detached way—to note the words he uses with other people, what behavior puts him at ease, and try to adopt his style when relating to him.

She contacted me a few weeks later to report some changes in their relationship. "I was able to observe that he felt most comfortable when people spoke to him in bottom line terms, and kept their comments short and to-the-point. He's very practical. So I began to relate to him in the same way. He seemed much more open to listening to what I had to say. I've also learned when to approach him. Early morning isn't a good time. But he hangs around the office after work, and he's open to talking then. My natural communication style is totally different than his. I'm more expressive and like to explore a situation from many perspectives, so it's been useful to learn how to adapt to another person's style."

As Sharon found out, another principle to help us communicate powerfully is the concept of "right timing." The words we say and the style we use have an impact but only if the people we want to reach are ready to hear us. So the time when we approach them must also be right.

I suggest that you find yourself a support buddy and review the principles of power communication: See the positive in a situation and speak it; Observe and honor the other person's style; Use their language to communicate effectively; Know the value of right timing. Agree to speak with each other briefly at least once a week to share positive and negative experiences.

"Networking is not a natural instinct for us. We haven't been doing it for that many years. I think the more protective we become of each other and each other's successes, the higher we will all soar."

—Paula Zahn, television anchor

Networking for Success

Networking is power, and the more we do it, the more successful we will become because we acquire more information and more contacts. Many of us know this to be true, yet we don't take the time to network. I hear resistance to networking all the time from women in my seminars: they say things like, "I'm doing the work for two people, how can I take time out to do more?" or "Most association meetings are in the evening, if I go to them, I'm taking time away from my family, who rarely see me to begin with." I understand these very real concerns. But I encourage my clients to carve out time in their already busy schedules to network because it is important to their careers.

I'm not the only one encouraging women to do this. Women

are getting the same message from different sources. Betsy, a marketing manager, was told by her boss, "Everyone knows your reports, but they don't know you. It is as important for you to make a reputation for yourself, get to know as many people as you can in the organization in informal settings. They learn to trust you that way and want you on their team. That's how you move up here."

Betsy acknowledged that she had to take action and did. She says, "At first, it felt uncomfortable—just schmoozing with people is not my style; I much prefer working in my office alone. But I've noticed that my relationships with my co-workers have become stronger, and people seem more friendly to me. Needless to say, my access to information has improved."

What are the skills of power networkers? They are good listeners and have a genuine interest in their co-workers. Mary is a good example. She is very busy, but never too busy to take a few moments out of her day to find out how the someone else person is. So when Mary needs information, the other person makes it a priority to get it for her. If you don't naturally have networking skills, there are a number of good seminars that can train you on the techniques of power networkers. I suggest you give one a try.

Everyone that you have been remotely involved with, from a college professor to your exercise trainer, is a potential networking contact. Yes, your friends, relatives, acquaintances, and business colleagues—they are all a source of information and advancement.

Networking has many benefits that will touch all areas of your life. Not only will you meet new people who can empower you to achieve some of your goals, but you will also gather many new ideas to tackle your current challenges at home and at work.

> *"Living in process is being open to insight and encounter.*
> *Creativity is becoming intensively absorbed in the process*
> *and giving it form."*
>
> —S. Smith

Cultivate Your Creative Power

Each of us has the ability to make something from nothing.
We can tap into our creative power by being attentive to what's
needed in the moment and acting accordingly, whatever form
that takes. For one woman, that might mean choreographing
the right people to attend an important meeting, to another it
means giving birth to productive ideas, and yet to another, it is
shopping for and preparing a sumptuous meal. Using our creative energy is what makes our lives vital. It turns the ordinary into extraordinary. And it allows us to transcend ruin and
decay.

   Lisa is a woman who has used her creativity to overcome a
tragic loss. She says, "A few nights ago, I woke up at 1:30 in
the morning because I heard screaming coming from the com-

munity beach and bath facility. I ran out of my house and saw the structure on fire. I called for help and the firemen came but most of the building had already burned to the ground. The families in our neighborhood were devastated by this disaster. The next day, one of the other residents came with me to inspect the ashes. We cried together, mourning our loss. To see the place that had given so many of us so much joy this summer, gone, was tragic. As a group, we had taken out insurance on the facility so there is money to rebuild it. I have decided to volunteer my services as part of the restoration committee. I am determined that we can build a new structure that will be even more functional than the old one. Some mothers have talked about adding a playground next to the bath house for small children. With the help of my neighbors, next summer we will not only have our beach house again, but a park, too."

Like Lisa, we can always tap into our creativity to deal with life's circumstances. Right now, let's do an experiment that I call Creative Observation so you can experience the ordinary become extraordinary:

Pick up a pen and hold it in front of you. See the texture of the pen. Take note of its different surfaces. Really look at it. If your mind starts wandering off, bring it back by observing the pen's colors. Do not allow yourself to get distracted. Keep your attention on the pen. Now, see if the pen has any other textures, colors or shapes that you hadn't noticed. As your attention gets more focused, the pen will seem to come alive.

When we view people, places, and things in our lives creatively, we experience them as if we were seeing them for the first time.

"Determined, fearless women are redefining glamour. It's their unremitting talent and smarts that make the difference now."

—Grace Mirabella, founder, *Mirabella* magazine

Claim Your Talents

In my late teens, I struggled with revealing my talent. However, I was mentored by a well-known photographer, Danielle, who encouraged me to explore my creative vision. We were talking one evening about my love of China. (Although, I've never visited the country, I've always been drawn to it. I find the ancient mysticism and Buddhist philosophy absolutely intriguing.) I had this wonderful idea to create a photographic exposé of China. Each photo would be round like a mandala and would be accompanied by Haiku poetry.

Danielle was excited by my idea and kept encouraging me to develop it. My art had never been taken seriously before. The fact that she saw my potential as a poet sparked my enthusiasm and I was inspired to write the poems. Working on this project was so much fun. It was as if a creative faucet had been opened, and the Haiku verses gushed out of me.

I was lucky to have a mentor to help me claim my artistic talent, but even if there has been no one in your life to encourage you, you can still make it a priority to discover what is uniquely yours to manifest.

For each of us the process is different. Linda Glick is a woman whom I admire because she has worked very seriously on developing her talents. She is a woman with a mission. As a result of her experiences with breast cancer in the last five years, she is now in the process of producing a one-woman show that will empower and educate women about the disease. For Linda, female power is the "intuition, mystery, and nurturing—the creative capacity that we all share." In her play, we experience Linda's voice, "in the spoken, written, and musical outpouring" of how she feels and how she hopes to move others from one point to another by sharing her own story.

Paula Zahn's commitment directs her actions. "I've never doubted what my agenda is and my agenda is pretty simple. I think I've been given a tremendous amount of responsibility to be on the air every day. I think in my own little way I can make people's lives better through providing health information or helping someone better understand a political issue."

We each have a unique contribution to make to this world. What is yours? In order to fully express our talents and to live with a clear sense of purpose, we must first discover what the range of our abilities are.

creating career &
personal visions

Men have traditionally held the reins on economic power which may have impacted our ideas about earning money and our ability to advance in our careers. I believe that it is possible to create a fulfilling career and economic security if you have a long-term vision, feel it's your right to achieve it, and are guided by smart people along the way.

Unfortunately, with our busy schedules, some of us don't take the time to explore our career visions, plan our next moves, and reach out for adequate support to make them happen. But if we are to achieve the positions of power we desire, then such reflection and evaluation is crucial.

The tools and insights that we gain about manifesting our career visions are transferable to our personal lives. This section will explore both career and personal visions from different perspectives.

> *"One morning you wake up and you know what you have to do and you find the courage to do it."*
>
> —H.L.R.

Believe in Yourself

A woman who has demonstrated economic power is Liz Claiborne. Liz went through many challenges when she opened her company with her husband, Art, but they were both determined to make it a successful venture. As she says, "Liz Claiborne Inc. was started with Art, when we had both been working in the industry for a long time. I was forty-seven and he was forty-nine. We had been successful at what we had individually done, and something happened in the company that I was working for that brought me to a stage in my career where I had to make a decision to stay on or to leave. It was kind of the perfect catalyst. We decided why not test our abilities, start from scratch and try to form a company that we believe in, that works the way we think a company should work. It was fantastically exciting to do it at that time. We did it with minimal funding so we did everything ourselves.

"We worked terribly hard, but it's so exciting starting your own thing that you're willing to do an awful lot that you wouldn't think you'd be willing to do. We couldn't afford a cleaning service so I did the cleaning at night. I helped in the showroom. We had one salesperson. That salesperson had been on her feet for two days and she said, 'Liz, it's your turn.' I'd never sold before, I'm a designer. I always liked to be in the background. Well, I discovered I could sell if I had to sell. So you can do all those kinds of things that you've never done before. It's a tremendous learning experience."

Liz had a sense that she could take the risk because even if it didn't work out, she had skills to fall back on. She felt strongly that in order to create change in your life you have to "believe in yourself, and work at it. That's another point women don't often realize—that is you have to work terribly hard at whatever you want to do. If you want to raise a family and have a career, you have to work doubly hard, be really dedicated and put in years of time that maybe you think you shouldn't have to. But you do, it all pays off."

Liz is living proof that if you desire to do something, you can achieve it with faith in yourself, lots of help, and hard work.

"To always opt for security keeps one stuck. "
—H.L.R.

Take Calculated Risks

I've noticed that one of the qualities successful people have in common is the ability to take calculated risks. Paula Bills started The Women's Forum at her company several years ago. She knew for a long time that women needed to converse more with each other in order to achieve greater professional and personal success. She decided that there was no "right" time, so she took a calculated risk and launched the group's first meeting. The group has been meeting successfully ever since.

When it comes to taking risks, we can learn a lot from children who, in general, are natural risk-takers. They are powerful because they believe they have a right to succeed and are unwilling to accept the limitations that grown-ups accept as reality. Recently, while at the playground with my son, we were stopped by three six-year-old girls who were selling their old toys. They had the faith that people would buy them and took the risk to set up "shop" outside the playground. I gave my son a dollar and encouraged him to pick out one of the stuffed animals. As we were about to leave, I told the girls to keep up the good work and walked away smiling. I had the feeling that I would be reading about one or all of them in the future. Who knows, maybe they'll be CEOs of corporations in the year 2040!

Taking calculated risks involves analyzing the pros and cons of a given action, and if the pluses outweigh the minuses, then you know it's an indication to take the next step. It's also useful to get feedback from others who have been in similar situations. If they've succeeded, you have a reasonable chance of succeeding too. Taking risks involves a certain amount of anxiety, so if you feel uneasy about following through on your decision, that's natural. Don't allow this uneasiness to deter you from pushing forward. When it comes to risk-taking, you will never get enough information to avoid feeling afraid; that's why it's risky. There is always a moment when you have to act, despite your fears, and jump out into the unknown.

"Change really becomes a necessity when we try not to do it."

—Anne Wilson Schaef

Accept Change

The one thing we can be certain about is that change is inevitable. Change is like a wave—we can't hold it back. By trying to resist the inevitable we are pulled under. But when we embrace it, we have the power to mobilize our resources to meet the challenge presented to us.

Change is frightening for many of us because when it happens our lives seem out of control. All the markers we have used to navigate disappear . . . and we don't know what is going to happen next. That's why both positive and negative changes are extremely stressful. For example, in changing jobs or living quarters, even if it is our choice, we still need to become accustomed to a new space, new people, and find the best places to eat—all at the same time.

Change can force us to take on new responsibilities. My friend Mary Jane was presented with many challenges as a result of a divorce and experienced tremendous growth. She result of a divorce and experienced tremendous growth. She says, "I was divorced about twenty years ago when my children were eight and twelve. At the time, my ex-husband thought I would disintegrate. We were living in Indiana, and he thought I would go back to my family in Georgia. However, I opted to stay and found a very good job as the director of volunteers at a hospital. A group of 350 volunteers reported to me. Then my biggest challenge was working a full-time job and raising two daughters. The younger one grew up in the '60s and '70s and you know what kind of time that was, so there were problems, but we pulled through all right."

How did Mary Jane find the power to take these risks? "The things that I've gone through in my life I could not have done if I didn't have a deep belief in God. A belief that it's going to come out fine in the end. You have to go through these things and your character doesn't grow unless you do have certain tests." Rather than lamenting the fact that her life had changed, Mary Jane was able to act from a position of strength and create a new life for her family and herself.

Changes in our lives can create the time and space to define and explore our career visions. What may have been an unwarranted change can turn out to be a opportunity in disguise.

"Desiring change is the first step toward changing."
—H.L.R.

Don't Get Sidetracked

Staying focused on what we want to accomplish is the key to exercising our power. This is difficult to do because of constant distractions. In the face of numerous obstacles, some of us may doubt our capabilities and our ability to change our circumstances. There are always dozens of reasons why we can't achieve a goal we want to reach but we must not pay attention to them. I've found over the years what has helped me with self-doubt is concentrating even harder on my objectives.

It is important that we learn to discriminate between the defeatist voices inside our heads and our desire to expand. The latter encourages us to seek new challenges, to go beyond what we know, to dream big and to make our visions happen.

Unfortunately, sometimes we don't listen to this counsel

and get stuck. This happened to Alice. She found it hard to stay focused on her career aspirations because she was afraid she would not be able to financially support her children. She had recently been given notice that she would be laid off in a year from her current job. She says, "I had planned to change careers from accounting to marketing and sales, but when my boss told me that my job would be eliminated next year, all I could think about was getting a job as an accountant somewhere else. I'm a single mother and no one else helps me out. The thought of losing my paycheck terrified me."

Alice had been with her company for thirteen years. Over the next few months, we had many conversations and strategized how she would approach searching for a new position. Her boss had been encouraging her to explore accounting jobs in other divisions of her company, as well as in other corporations. Now she is taking the first steps to do so. In fact, she has been given time off to go on interviews. In addition, I have suggested that she also take an evening course in marketing at a nearby college and attend meetings of a local sales organization. She has committed to take these action steps too.

Because of the encouragement Alice has received from her friends, she is determined not to get sidetracked and will continue to take steps toward achieving her career vision.

"Power is claiming a direction for yourself. As females, we need to pursue our talents, taking charge and claiming what we think we can do."

—Adele Scheele, Ph.D., author of
Career Strategies for the Working Woman

Recognize Past Accomplishments

Traditionally women are excellent managers because of our ability to juggle several projects at once and get our work done efficiently. But some of us fall short when it comes to planning for ourselves and our future. We can learn a lot from certain of our male colleagues about the importance of long-range career planning. They view taking actions towards creating their future success as a top priority. It is as important as doing their current job. In other words, they view jobs as just rungs on their career ladder to be used to get to the next level.

Perhaps underneath our very real concerns of juggling responsibilities and finding time for self-advancement is fear. We may doubt if our career goals will ever materialize so we do not take the necessary actions to achieve them. But we should not let our fears stop us from fully expressing our abilities as workers. I've learned that I can be afraid and move ahead anyway.

For those of us in need of support, let me help you start the process of planning your career growth. Here's an exercise that many experts have used to build confidence. It points out how much you've probably already achieved.

Make a list of your accomplishments and skills at different ages, starting with your twenties. For example, "In my twenties, I was a salesperson for a publishing company and won a paid vacation as the top sales rep." (accomplishment); "Good people skills enabled me to achieve this." (skills). Continue to inventory your accomplishments and skills for your thirties, forties, fifties and so on.

Now read the list through and really recognize what you have accomplished and what skills you possess. Don't throw this list away, but refer to it when you need to bolster your confidence. Acknowledging your past and present successes will help you create your future career moves. Remember, "growing a career" takes time and involves a process of discovery. You must have a realistic picture of where you have been (complete with all your successes) in order to move forward.

"As we meet more people and begin to formulate our career vision, we become more confident in marketing our strengths."

—H.L.R.

Build Your Career Vision

Creating a career vision is a process that has many different steps. Start by taking small actions. For example, besides listing all of your accomplishments as was just suggested, make it a part of your work week to interview at least one person who is doing something related to what you think you would ultimately like to do.

Sarah, who has successfully gone through this process shared with me, "It was very useful. Most of these encounters were stimulating. To my surprise, people were flattered by my interest in them. I was able to do my current job better because I had access to more people and information. I'm also getting a better sense of a possible career path and long-range vision by hearing those of other people. I even spoke with one woman who told me about a position, and I will interview for it next week."

The process of creating your future work is very exciting. It is essential for you to be flexible along the way, because your life circumstances may change and alter your goals. Consider this scenario: Your children are still young, so you don't want a job that would involve 80 percent travel. Fifteen years later, that may be precisely what entices you.

Vision Builders

- Read trade publications and newspapers with an eye on women who have successfully created their career vision. Note how they've gotten there and what about their career appeals to you.

- Join a networking group and get to know lots of women who, like you, want to make a difference in business. Find out who they are and where they are going.

- Be realistic in setting goals for yourself, but don't feel that any goal is out of reach. Something that is not possible today may be your next step tomorrow.

"My favorite thing is to go where I've never been."
—Diane Arbus

Make It Happen

Everyone has the power to realize his or her vision. My friend Sally is an example. She is in her late thirties and runs a successful business, but has never owned property. Last year, she discovered her hidden desire to build her own home.

Sally was about to close on a house, but the engineer who surveyed the property told her that it wasn't worth the price the owner was asking for it. He let her know about a parcel of land which was available that was part of an old estate that had been subdivided. They went to look at it and Sally fell in love with the line of old trees on the property that had been planted by the original owner. All the shrubbery on the lot was overgrown. It had been neglected for years. That didn't stop Sally from envisioning the land cleared and where her log cabin would be built. She bought the property the next day and negotiated a fair price for it. Sally saw the potential in the property, which was the first step in creating her dream log cabin home.

The next step in manifesting her home was to hire the right people to build the house. Sally felt confident that after asking for referrals, she'd find the right crew for the job. Of course, her feelings ran the gamut of fear, terror, and excitement. Her network of women friends kept encouraging her to go for it. And she did.

Like Sally, we each have the capacity to make things happen that we want in our lives. It's a matter of acknowledging a hidden desire, seeing the potential in a situation and having confidence in our ability to bring it about.

Look to see if there is something in your life that you have wanted to create but you have put off doing, for whatever reason. Actually write down what it is and why you have not done it, i.e., I want to take a vacation out of the country but I haven't done it because I can't save enough money after paying my monthly expenses. Now, ask yourself, is the only reason that I haven't taken a trip abroad because of money? Really probe for other reasons. Perhaps, you have not planned a foreign trip because you would be spending a lot of time alone— most of your friends are married and would not be able to go with you.

To counteract your resistance and fears, visualize the details of a possible trip. Be as specific as possible. Imagine where you would go and what you would want to do. For instance, "I want to go to Africa because I have read so much about it. I want to take a safari to see wild tigers and lions. I want to travel with a friend who will love the adventure and sights as much as I will."

Now that you have envisioned yourself there, write down the necessary steps to make it happen. Some of them might be to brainstorm with a friend about additional ways to save money; go to a travel agent to pick up some brochures about safaris; attend some meetings of a travel club to increase your contacts of possible travel partners. Then, start planning when the trip will happen, give it a specific date, and calculate the duration and the estimated costs.

Making our visions happen is a powerful process. If we allow ourselves to take actions that make our visions specific and believable, it is quite probable that they will materialize.

> *"The sooner you start getting some of what you really want, the more energy you'll have to go for the rest of it!"*
>
> —Barbara Sher and Anne Gottlieb,
> authors of *Wishcraft*

A Taste for Empowerment

What it takes to keep creating our lives powerfully is to acknowledge each day that we are the source of our power. And it is up to us to take the appropriate actions in order to attain what we want. It's so easy to fall back and think that circumstances have been responsible for our fortune or misfortune, but this type of thinking is deceptive. We have choices about how we want to live our lives, and every day we make decisions which create our reality.

I go in and out of remembering this and rely on my female friends to remind me when I forget. For example, I knew I needed to take a few weeks off last summer to play with Heath, my son. Due to a heavy work schedule last year, he didn't see as much of me as he might have wanted to. So a vacation was in order, but I felt obligated to finish certain projects. I have a wonderful network of friends who advised me to rent a summer house for the month of August and vacation with Heath there. Even though I felt pressured by my obligations, I took their advice and found a magical house right near the water. I'm actually there as I write this piece, receiving divine inspiration from the swans gliding on the lake outside my window. (Heath is at a nearby camp for the mornings and we play together at the water's edge in the afternoons.) So with a little help from my friends, I was able to create exactly what Heath and I needed.

Exercising our power is the essence of intimacy with oneself. Those limitations that we impose upon ourselves, such as the work that must get done or the time we do not have, blocks us from living fully. How can we open up more to create what we need for ourselves and our loved ones? One way is to visualize a time when we actually created what we wanted. Just like I did with my summer house!

power
expanders

unity among women

Our power is greatly expanded when we support one another, both at work and in our personal lives. As one of us faces a seemingly impossible challenge, or achieves some new goal, or struggles with the process of discovery, we all benefit. By sharing our experiences with each other, we get stronger both individually and as a group, and we pave the way for those who will come after us.

> *"As we give fully, unafraid to let others know the truth about ourselves, we receive unexpected rewards from unexpected sources."*
>
> —H.L.R.

Solidarity and Sisterhood

MARIANNE WILLIAMSON, *author and lecturer*

The love we show must extend to one another. When my first book was published, I appeared as a guest on Oprah Winfrey's television show. As we sat in front of the cameras, I heard Oprah praise my book and tell the audience that she herself had bought a thousand copies. From that point on, it became a bestseller. Due to Oprah's generosity and enthusiasm that day, my professional life took a giant step forward.

While it is true that Oprah has tremendous power and influence, I realized upon reflection that every woman can be an Oprah to someone. Imagine what the world would be like if every woman showed support to at least one other woman, standing behind her in some way on the ladder of success. Oprah seems to have the desire to share with others what she has received, and I would imagine this consciousness is part of her huge success. What she demonstrated to me was the power of sisterhood, where a woman helps another woman and others are helped in the process.

We must not fail to learn from the lessons of women who share their bounty of opportunity and influence and power and goodwill. There is a mountaintop with enough room for all of us. None of us will get there and stay there unless all of us get there and stay there. If women succeed only in isolated cases, the professional world will continue to be unsure ground for women in general. We must take the communion of women very seriously at this time and do all we can do to support other women in reaching for the stars. There cannot be too many glorious women. There cannot be too many queens. There cannot be too much success.

There's a lot of talk today about whether a woman can have it all. The problem isn't having it all but receiving it all, giving ourselves permission to have a full and passionate life when our cultural conditioning has denied us that for centuries. The biggest limit to our having is our small reach, our shy embrace. As long as it's considered unfeminine to have a full appetite—which it is, because it is recognized that whatever we allow ourselves to truly desire we usually get—then we will not sit down at life's banquet but only at its diner. This is ridiculous, and it holds back the entire world for women to live at half-measure. It's also an insult to men to suggest that they can't dance with goddesses, as though a woman at full power might step on their toes.

For some men, perhaps, she is too much of a threat, but not for all of them. Men are changing just as we are, and together we are widening the path of emotional opportunity for women. This is our biggest block to power: the embarrassed looks when we express ourselves, the feeling in the room that we've gone too far whenever we've pushed any envelopes that matter. Men have got to realize—and so have we—that something of ancient significance is rising up from the bottom of things and spilling out through all of us. Men feel it; women feel it. Women, however, are going crazy around it because our nervous systems are tied to its expression. It's a pregnancy we can't abort, and when we try to, we get even crazier than we were. We might as well accept the fact that nature is turning the world on its ear, and she's chosen us to announce the news.

—*excerpt from* A Woman's Worth

"She became for me an island of light, fun, wisdom where I could run with my discoveries and torments and hopes at any time of the day and find welcome."

—May Sarton

A Special Kind of Friendship

Together, women with similar stresses and challenges can support each other to move ahead. What's wonderful about female friendships is that everybody wins. On a day that I feel down, you encourage me to rise up. But I, in turn, am there for you when you need to be reminded about your potential for success. And on the days we both need a lift, we can let the other person know and agree to respect each other's limitations.

Sarah and Janet have a special relationship. Sarah says about Janet, "I certainly never experienced the kind of compassion and coaching Janet gives me. We listen to each other a lot. Yes, we get into arguments, but they don't seem to last very long. We've supported each other to move forward in our lives. Just recently, I was to deliver a presentation to top management in my company, and I came down with a bad cold. I felt miserable and was sure I would not do my best. Of course, I called Janet and complained. Left to my own devices, I would have canceled the meeting. But Janet advised me not to go to the gym that night and go to sleep early. She had faith that I'd be fine the next day. Armed with tissues, my report, and Janet's good advice, I showed up for the meeting. I felt shaky but didn't look it. Despite an occasional sneeze, everything went as planned. Thank God it was Friday. I crashed that night and slept all weekend."

I was recently with my sister and she was talking about how in the last three years, she hasn't gotten together with her female friends on a regular basis. They used to go out together as a group at least once a month. Between work and family responsibilities, nobody has the time, and she really misses them. I believe female friendships are a necessity. Something special happens when women come together informally to play or bare their souls that doesn't seem to happen when men are present. Other women can give us feedback that puts our own problems into perspective. And we have an opportunity to release pent-up feelings about our work and family relationships.

Even with the busiest of people, there's always time for those things that we judge important!

> *"Caring deepens our commitment to other women and provides a vehicle for support, encouragement, and recognition of our worth."*
>
> —Carolyn Duff, author of
> *When Women Work Together*

Bond with Other Women

When we are under tremendous stress at work, we sometimes fragment our power by getting caught up in the "worker" role we are playing, and take on behavior that isn't consistent with how we act in other areas of our lives. We may not acknowledge a job well done in ourselves or others, or take the time to find out how our co-workers are doing. Under pressure, there is a tendency to be fearful, and fear has a spiraling effect. We feel constricted, losing our sense of generosity with each other. (And then we wonder why our jobs aren't more satisfying!)

Some working women have found it particularly difficult to bond with other women because they are fiercely competing for too few jobs at senior management levels. They feel, "Why should I help you get the job that I'm slated for?" Yet in their personal lives, they may behave quite differently with their female friends because they've learned the value of these relationships. But bonding with other women at work doesn't necessarily mean helping them take our place. There are numerous ways that women can support one another without jeopardizing their own positions, for instance: providing each other with networking contacts, giving feedback about a challenging situation and the results that were achieved, commiserating about child care and elder care, sponsoring a new member for a trade association, or exchanging information about industry trends.

In the future, women will be in a position to advance other women as never before. In *Megatrends for Women,* futurists John Naisbitt and Patricia Aburdene describe the concept of "critical mass"—that by the year 2000, a great many women will have entered the workforce, making it inevitable for more of us to rise to top level positions.

As women leaders, we have an opportunity to build our own teams, to shape the marketplace, and to lead with our own management style. We need to cultivate and reciprocate to the women coming into the workforce today who are demanding our guidance and expertise. A Queen Bee (a woman who hoards her success and doesn't give back) can no longer survive in a workplace with an increasing number of women.

"Creative Aggression is defined as taking initiative; leading others; speaking out and expressing autonomous opinions . . ."

—Dorothy W. Cantor and Toni Bernay,
authors of *Women in Power*

Abandon the Myths

ANDREA ZINTZ, *vice president of human resources, Ortho Biotech, Inc.*

Powerful women have learned to draw upon the power that men have, and go underground to influence decisions and events in their favor. This is evidenced by the strong but quiet roles many mothers have played in families—families where the father was seen as king of the household, but the mother held the "real" power.

This "covert" form of power doesn't look very impressive from the outside. But in actuality it works very well. These "guerrilla" women act polite, selfless, and passive, but nonetheless manage to "wrap the men in the family around their little fingers." They have learned how to work this way from the models their mothers and other powerful women in their lives have set for them.

Many women carry this way of working with power into business. However, it has a serious pitfall. Drawing upon the power of men means attributing power to those men. By giving power to men, women put themselves in the position of reacting and responding, rather than initiating. This reinforces a false assumption—held by men and women alike—that, as women, we are not powerful, even though we may influence decisions and events quite expertly.

We must use our powers of self-discovery to see the power we hold within ourselves. We must confront our tendencies to yield power to others. And we must decide that we will change that.

This change will not be easy. We must learn to be more direct, without being hurtful and insensitive. We must not be so nice and polite when niceness reflects a lack of purpose, and when politeness indicates an unwillingness to face difficult confrontations. We must choose to take the reins of power ourselves when we are the best person for the job—not empower a male co-worker who may have fewer abilities for the task.

We must also mentor other women to challenge the old

societal assumptions and myths, in part by encouraging them to use the principle of the eccentricity ratio; that is, you can be as different as you are perceived to be credible. Women must help other women to operate strategically in their work relationships to attain this credibility without compromising their identity and reinforcing old stereotypes.

It is difficult for women to actively support other women who take risks to challenge the old power paradigms. Too often, when a man is appropriately challenged in public by a woman, another woman will rise to defend him!

Complex issues? You bet! These complexities underscore our need for self-discovery, for joining with other women to face what we've given up, for confronting the myths we've taken as truth.

We must confront our own biases to understand, to learn from, and to support women of other races and other ethnic groups. We must acquire new skills: skills such as learning to silence the internal voices that tell us to be quiet and fit into the corporate roles we have been assigned; skills that enable us to assert our identities through competence and confidence; skills that help us understand how to play the game, while keeping our power rather than giving it away.

—written for this book

"Competition, taken too far, can get in the way of a healthy and positive climate overall."

—Ann M. Morrison, Randall P. White, Ellen Van Velsor, authors of *Breaking The Glass Ceiling*

Cooperate & Compete

How can we support each other as women? One way is by working together to create new ground rules for competing with one another. In the last few years, I have witnessed the growth of corporate women's groups across the United States. Some of them have formed around the critical business issues that confront their companies or industries. Whatever reason brings these women together, they are finding that by sharing strategies they become not only an important resource to their companies, but also increase their individual chances for upward mobility.

The size, structure, and purpose of these groups varies. Some of them are restricted to company employees, whereas others include members from different organizations within an industry. Other groups draw their membership from diverse industries. These women meet to offer each other tips and information without jeopardizing their companies' respective competitive advantages.

Here's how one group makes it work: I was privileged to be the keynote speaker at a group called the Grocery Manufacturers Of America, Test Kitchen Roundtable, and was truly impressed by the women there. I arrived early, and sitting around the room were senior women from the major packaged goods companies. Fundamentally competitors, they were actively formulating strategies to take back to their respective companies that would ensure the meaningful contributions of corporate test kitchens around the country. However, these women were brainstorming with each other while guarding the proprietary nature of their respective businesses.

As a group, they had worked out what information they could and would not share, thereby respecting each other's boundaries. They knew the importance of teaming but did not discount their individual corporate ties. For example, one woman shared a strategy that was used to attain information about her brand, but when it came to revealing the actual results of the research, she refrained.

If you are not involved in a women's group that supports your career aspirations, you ought to be. Investigate a few of these groups by attending open meetings. Joining with your female colleagues can be both validating and exhilarating. By clarifying your boundaries and sharing with other women, you will empower each other's success without risking your own.

> *"I have met brave women who are exploring the outer edge of possibility, with no history to guide them and a courage to make themselves vulnerable that I find moving beyond the words to express it."*
>
> —Gloria Steinem, preview issue of *Ms.* magazine, 1972

The Power of Diversity

ANN RICHARDS, *former Governor of Texas*

I hope you're not going to give in to . . . cynicism. Back when dinosaurs roamed the earth and I was your age, politics was a male province. Women made the coffee and men made the decisions. But now that men have learned to make coffee and a few of us are in decision-making positions, it would be a calamity if you turn away just when you can make the most difference, just when you can be the difference between a system that collapses under its own tired weight and a system that is rejuvenated by new ideas, new blood, new faces. . . .

I am not suggesting to you that [women] are needed in the corridors of power because we're going to make different decisions about the stereotypical women's issues like sexual harassment and parental leave. Nor am I suggesting that only women are qualified to deal with those issues. What I am saying is that because our background is different, we pick up different nuances and bring valuable skills to the process.

And Lord knows, we could not do worse than is being done now.

Perhaps because we have been watching the show as spectators for so long, we are less likely to get caught up in the trappings and the ceremony. We're not there for the honor of it. We are there to do a job. We are more likely to understand that we are not one bit smarter the day after we are elected than we were the day before. And because we are not vested in the status quo, we are more likely to ask the impertinent and crucial questions.

My favorite one is, "why are we doing this this way?" Of course, the predictable answer is, "because we have always done it that way." Well, that's not good enough.

The real question for women, and for minorities, and for all of us who have been excluded in the past, is what difference our public service will make. . . .

In an incredibly short period of time, we have moved from watching at the end of the procession, and now we move with our brothers to the head of the procession and to leadership.

And what . . . are our terms?

Of the procession, we ask only that our perspective as women be valued. But of ourselves, we must ask more: that our participation makes our society more just, makes it more humane, and makes our government more determined to meet the needs of all human beings who live in it.

—*excerpt from Smith College Commencement Address*

"There is a continuum of strength, flowing from one generation to another."

—H.L.R.

Power in Numbers

BARBARA B. KENNELLY, *Congresswoman*

Women are achieving greater success—and in the success of ourselves and of our sisters, all of our confidence has grown, grown in our values, our views of how our world might be. There is power in our numbers, and as individuals we are bolder in expressing our special perspective. We have greater confidence to cast our votes according to our own paradigms of leadership, of morality, of thought.

Feminist scholars have started to chart the female norm of moral and intellectual development. Harvard psychologist Carol Gilligan, in her study of moral conflict and choice, has found that young girls consistently approached and solved problems in a way that was different than young boys. The girls spoke in a "different voice." The girls saw a moral problem in all its facets. They saw in every action the ramifications on the lives of the people faced with conflict. The feminine view or paradigm sees moral problems in all their complexity. In the feminine norm of moral development, issues are rarely cut and dried. Actions have ramifications far beyond their immediate context.

Still, for Gilligan, one voice is not superior to another; each is different. Both are necessary. But for too long, the female voice has been discounted, ignored, considered the voice outside the norm.

Today is a new day. Gilligan makes the point, and I would suggest to you that these feminine paradigms of leadership are critical to our civilization at the present moment. We must solve problems by diplomacy, by our acute awareness of our connection with each other, with an awareness of the illusion of isolation. We must address the problems facing our government and our society by taking into account the problems in all their facets, in all their ramifications affecting people's lives.

Please do not think I am making the point that we need to have more of a "woman's touch." Please do not interpret my remarks to mean that I am trying to resurrect some nineteenth-century stereotype of women being better than men, angels posed on pedestals. Rather, I simply note that women, perhaps because of our long history of being powerless, do seem to have a different attitude toward power, an attitude that must be learned by all people who live in this nuclear age, an attitude that goes beyond the traditional male concept that every conflict reaches resolution when there is a winner and a loser. In nuclear conflict, there are no winners, only losers.

I see the goal for women to synthesize within society the best character traits of femininity and masculinity as ideal human traits, without denying our individual differences. I see the goal to incorporate into our society the values of compassion, the worth of the family, the dignity of the individual and the protection of those who cannot help themselves. I see the goal to encourage personal fulfillment, to tap energy and ambition, to provide fertile ground for excellence for women and for all people.

To reach these goals we must work hard, being conscious at the same time that we do not succeed alone. We touch the stars by standing on the shoulders of the giants who have gone before us. And to you who come after us, we give a hand.

—excerpt from Mt. Holyoke College Commencement Address

love as power

Love is one of the greatest power expanders there is, for it
brings us together on behalf of each other, makes us see
unity in conflict, and forges bridges where there were none.
Under the stress of everyday life, particularly in our quest
to expand our power, we sometimes forget our natural im-
pulse to love, which is always there. It needs only to be
rediscovered.

> *"Love can never be depleted because it grows inside of us. But we must take quiet, nurturing time to honor ourselves. To ask ourselves who we are. By honoring ourselves, we'll find our power."*
>
> —Susan Taylor, editor-in-chief, *Essence* magazine

The Art of Love

Love is a dynamic force that requires us to honor ourselves and those around us. For example, when we are aware of our needs and take time to nurture ourselves, we love. When we set boundaries and define what we can and cannot do for others, we love. When we are attentive to others and give without strings attached, we love.

Loving involves respecting the differences between people. They need not think as we do, say what we say or feel the way we do. We realize that their point of view is just as valid as our own. When we love, we experience a connectedness to all living beings and a power greater than ourselves. As Melody Beattie reveals in *The Language of Letting Go,* "We are free to listen to the gentle, loving words of a Higher Power, words whispered to and through each of us."

For many of us loving freely is a new experience. As we love, we separate from old, destructive habits. In his book *Loving Each Other,* Leo Buscaglia suggests, "to bring another into our life in love we must be willing to give up certain destructive characteristics. For example:

The need to be always right.
The need to be first in everything.
The need to be constantly in control.
The need to be perfect.
The need to be loved by everyone.
The need to possess.
The need to be free of conflict and frustration.
The need to change others for our needs.
The need to manipulate.
The need to blame.
The need to dominate."

Change is never easy, even when the rewards are great. But with support we can learn to love in a new way. Whether our guide is a therapist, or other caring friends, or a more formal women's group, these significant others are available to all of us if we reach out to them.

"To err is human, to forgive divine."

—Alexander Pope

Practice Forgiveness

Exercising our power involves forgiving those people who have let us down. For example, Jane's mother was very jealous of her and undermined her talents when she was growing up. Jane joined a women's group at her church, and over the past few years has been able to get the support to value her abilities more, express her feelings of anger toward her mother, and accept and forgive her mother's shortcomings.

There's a great release of energy and resources as we forgive people from our past who may have hurt us. This spills over into all our relationships at home and on the job. Instead of trying to prove how "right" we are by fighting an old battle that has not been resolved, we have the opportunity to become more intimate. My friend Barbara knows this to be true. She had an unhappy childhood and has worked through many of her feelings about her overbearing father with a therapist. She recently told me how she resisted arguing with her husband (who reminds her of her father). She reported, "My husband was going to take my son to the movies and I was going to a business meeting. He wanted to discuss how we would handle the car arrangements. He asked me what I thought and I told him. I suggested that he take my son to an early movie, come back with the car, and then I would go out to my meeting. He listened and responded, 'It's always your agenda.' I could feel every ounce of me wanting to reply nastily. (And I have many times.) After all, he asked me what I thought. And besides, just the other day I had gone out of my way for him, so why couldn't he do the same for me? Well, I took a long deep breath, remembered that he wasn't my father (who always wanted to be right), and realized that my arguing with my husband would get me no place, and then walked out of the room. As I left, I said calmly, 'Handle it any way you want to.' After five minutes, he came into the bedroom where I was reading and said that he would go to an early movie, and be back with the car as I had asked. Now, if I had argued with him, he would have never acted this way, and my son would have been uncomfortable hearing us fight."

Forgiveness is a powerful act. The process of forgiveness releases our power. As we forgive others, we become freer and more effective because we are not living our lives as a result of past injuries or injustices but choosing who we want to be in the present.

"Our relationships and the situations we find ourselves in are reflections of how we feel about ourselves."

—H.L.R.

Conscious Living

MARIANNE WILLIAMSON, *author and lecturer*

Usually when we think of power, we think of external power, and we think of powerful people as those who have made it in the world. A powerful woman isn't necessarily someone who has money, but we think of her as someone with a boldness or a spark that makes her manifest in a dramatic way. When we think of a powerful man, we think of his ability to manifest abundance—usually money—in the world.

Most people say that a powerful woman does best with a powerful man, that she needs someone who understands the bigness of her situation, a man who can meet her on the same or a greater level of power in the world. This is true if power is defined as material abundance. A woman often faces cultural prejudice when she makes more money than a man, as does he. A woman who defines power by worldly standards can rarely feel totally relaxed in the arms of a man who doesn't have it.

If power is seen as an internal matter, then the situation changes drastically. Internal power has less to do with money and worldly position and more to do with emotional expansiveness, spirituality, and conscious living. As we begin to recognize that internal strength is all that really matters, we come to see that we have often avoided men who were not powerful in the world not because they were not powerful enough, but because inwardly they were too powerful, reminding us of the work we still had to do on ourselves.

I used to think that I needed a "powerful man," someone who could protect me from the harshness and evils of the world. What I have come to realize is that the evils of the world that confront me are a reflection of my own internal state, and no one can protect me from my own mind. The powerful man I was looking for would be, foremost, someone who supported me in keeping on track spiritually and in so maintaining clarity within myself that life would pose fewer problems. When it did get rough, he would help me forgive.

I no longer want someone who would say to me, "Don't worry, honey. If they're mean to you, I'll beat them up or buy them out." Instead, I want someone who prays and meditates with me regularly so that fewer monsters from the outer world disturb me, and who, when they do, helps me look within my own consciousness for answers instead of looking to false power to combat false power.

There's a big difference between a gentle man and a weak man. Weak men make us nervous. Gentle men make us calm.

—*excerpt from* A Woman's Worth

"To be somebody, a woman does not have to be more like a man, but has to be more of a woman."

—Dr. Sally E. Shaywitz

A Challenge for Powerful Women

MARY PARISH, *consultant and author*

A lot is being written lately about what happened to the women's movement. Are we done? Where have all the issues gone? Who are our leaders? What should we be about now, at the turn of the century?

I think we women could be doing what we were born to do. We could be claiming our birthright as women by bringing healthy, feminine energy into our work lives. We have spent years masquerading as men in order to gain power in a masculine world. Some of us have succeeded in that. Now what? Do we offer more of the same, in a slightly higher tone of voice? Now that we have gained some measure of power, it is time to re-connect with the feminine side of our psyche that we had to abandon to be taken seriously in this masculine culture. We can learn to accept conflict without sacrificing intimacy. In fact, we can use conflict and its resolution to deepen intimacy. We can use disagreement over ideas to build more solid and respectful working relationships. We can laugh while taking our work seriously. We can be strong individuals and committed group members. . . .

We women who have achieved power in these times, in these male organizational cultures, are now the ones who can bring about the consolidation and balance between the masculine and the feminine in organizations. Our journey through the male "battlefield" has changed us. Through a process of alchemy, we now have a better understanding about what is good in masculine approaches to the world.

Now, wherever we are in the journey, let us stop, pause and look inside ourselves, for that deep well of feminine energy, intelligence, and understanding. . . . We need to go inside, find our feminine truth, and reclaim our feminine power so we can bring it into a world that desperately needs it.

We are involved in important work on behalf of all women. If we don't do it, no one else will. We are capable.

We must not miss this opportunity to help balance the masculine approaches we have learned with the feminine approaches we know as a way of bringing the power of greater harmony to our workplaces, our communities, and our world. The time is now and the people are us.

—*excerpt from* "A Challenge for Powerful Women"

the bottom line

In the final analysis, it is knowing that we are free to choose among alternatives that makes us powerful. Although, we may be pleased with some of our choices and not others, no choice is irrevocable. As vital women, we can reach out for support and alter the course of our lives.

> *"So often I have listened to everyone else's truth and tried to make it mine. Now, I am listening deep inside for my own voice, and I am softly, yet firmly, speaking my truth."*
>
> —Liane Cordes

Dare to Claim Your Life

OLYMPIA DUKAKIS, *actress*

The issues of individual growth that confront us in our personal lives today exist within a larger picture. In this larger picture, the challenge to realize partnership relationships not only with men but with other women has emerged as a movement that is part of an underlying thrust to transform a system based on domination [in] to one that supports and nurtures partnerships with men and collaboration with women. . . .

Many of you know and have felt what it is to be silenced, to be abused, to be given less pay for equal work; to have your needs, your thoughts, your bodies, your dreams, ridiculed and trivialized—to obey others against your better judgment, to suppress qualities others find unacceptable and threatening—especially the sexual, independent, and outspoken parts of your personalities.

As a group, women have been trained not to act. We can "know" things, but have not really been encouraged or supported to act from this knowledge. Are we ready for partnership, are we going to choose to learn to move, to act, to do what our inner voices tell us we need to do? . . .

The courage and determination to claim our lives, however we wish to live them, is at the heart of the matter. To honor the spirit within that seeks to know and realize itself is at the heart of the matter. To value the consciousness that reaches out to nurture and love is at the heart of the matter. To raise the voice that can and will speak up, changing and shaping the lives of young people is at the heart of the matter.

There is a vision, a challenge, of sorts, for the '90s that will become increasingly more apparent as we actively and intelligently create the work we want, the workplace we want, the families we want, the lifestyle we want.

—excerpted from a speech given at the Women's Expo, Minnesota

"I discovered I always have choices and sometimes it's only a choice of attitude."

—Judith Knowlton

The Power of Choice

BARBARA BUSH, *former First Lady*

Decisions are not irrevocable. Choices do come back.... I hope that many of you [young women] will consider making three very special choices.

The first is to believe in something larger than yourself ... to get involved in some of the big ideas of our time. I chose literacy because I honestly believe that if more people could read, write, and comprehend, we would be that much closer to solving so many of the problems that plague our nation and our society.

Early on I made another choice which I hope you will

make as well. Whether you are talking about education, career or service, you are talking about life . . . and life really must have joy. It's supposed to be fun!

One of the reasons I made the most important decision of my life . . . to marry George Bush . . . is because he made me laugh. It's true, sometimes we've laughed through our tears . . . but that shared laughter has been one of our strongest bonds. Find the joy in life, because as Ferris Bueller said on his day off, ". . . Life moves pretty fast. You don't stop and look around once in a while you're gonna miss it! . . ."

The third choice that must not be missed is to cherish your human connections: your relationships with family and friends. For several years, you've had impressed upon you the importance to your career of dedication and hard work, and, of course, that's true. But as important as your obligations as a doctor, lawyer, or business leader will be, you are a human being first and those human connections—with spouses, with children, with friends—are the most important investments you will ever make. At the end of your life, you will never regret not having passed one more test, not winning one more verdict or not closing one more deal. You will regret time not spent with a husband, a child, a friend, or a parent.

We are in a transitional period right now . . . learning to adjust to the changes and the choices we . . . men and women . . . are facing. As an example, I remember what a friend said, on hearing her husband complain to his buddies that he had to babysit. Quickly setting him straight . . . my friend told her husband that when it's your own kids . . . it's not called babysitting!

Maybe we should adjust faster, maybe we should adjust slower. But whatever the era . . . whatever the times, one thing will never change: fathers and mothers, if you have children—they must come first. You must read to your children, hug your children, and you must love your children. Your success as a family . . . our success as a society depends not on what happens in the White House, but on what happens inside your house.

For over fifty years, it was said that the winner of Wellesley [College]'s annual hoop race would be the first to get married. Now they say the winner will be the first to become a CEO. Both of those stereotypes show too little tolerance for those who want to know where the mermaids stand. So I want to offer you today a new legend: the winner of the hoop race will be the first to realize her dream . . . not society's dreams . . . her own personal dream. And who knows? Somewhere out in this audience may even be someone who will one day follow in my footsteps, and preside over the White House as the President's spouse. I wish him well!

—*excerpt from Wellesley College Commencement Address*

"I alone cannot achieve what we can do together."
—Unknown

Ask for Help

The bottom line of many of the essays that you've read is that you don't have to do it alone. We're all in this together and you can ask for help. Powerful women know this. They've challenged their fear of appearing vulnerable and looking bad—not having it "all together." You see, they know no one does!

Asking for help takes many forms. It's reaching out to a colleague and asking for some career advice—guidance about how to get a step-up in salary, for example. It's talking with a fellow commuter about how she's managed to juggle all her responsibilities one more day. It's calling a neighbor to ask her to look after your child because your babysitter has to leave and you're stuck at work. It's asking colleagues and friends for referrals for child care and elder care. It's confiding in a friend about how your teenage daughter is going through growing pains, and you're about to pull your hair out and hers. It's being willing to get a sitter on a night when no one seems available so you can go out with your husband or have some "alone" time to replenish. The list goes on and on.

Of course, the women in our lives can be a great source of strength (if we seek them out). But we need also to reach out to men, at home and at the office. You'd be amazed how much help is available if we just ask for it.

It is by keeping our power circulating that we *all* claim it.

index

G
gender roles, 16-20

I
Ireland, Patricia, 24

K
Keller, Evelyn Fox, 98
Kennelly, Barbara B., 154
Kunin, Madeleine M., 79

L
leadership, 24-25, 79-81
Lowey, Nita M., 29

M
mentors, 89-91

N
networking, 107-109
National Organization for Women, 24

O
Oprah, 136-138

P
Parish, Mary, 166
passion, 101-102
perfectionism, 44-46, 52-54
planning, 124-125
play, 71-72
power
    covert v. overt, 145-147
    definition, 10-12, 21-23
    economic, 26-28

acknowledgments

In rereading the finished manuscript, I am lifted to a new level of awareness by the words and stories of the inspiring women in this book. My thanks to them and members of their staffs.

Thank you to Marjorie Vincent, my special friend and former colleague. Together, we created some of the ideas and exercises in this book for mentoring, power networking, and vision planning/business strategies for women.

Mary Jane Ryan, my publisher and editor, a woman who demonstrates the results of fully using her power because she is a co-creator of Conari Press: I thank you for your talents and skills. Many others deserve thanks for their insights and support. Cheri Wilczek, Joy Dargent, Liz and Victoria M. Stoneman, Susan Braun, Suzanne Altfeld, Susan Levin-Epstein, and Richard Greene.

Thanks to all of the women who have attended my workshops and lectures, watched and participated in my videos and television programs. You are powerful examples of women who have the desire and the ability to realize their visions.

Thanks to Heath Matthew Robbins, my five-year-old son, for his tenacity in making sure that I find a way to "juggle" it all every day. I love him dearly.

permissions acknowledgments

The author gratefully acknowledges permission to excerpt from the following:

From *A Woman's Worth* by Marianne Williamson. Copyright © 1993 by Marianne Williamson. Reprinted by permission of Random House, Inc.. Excerpt from "A Challenge for Powerful Women" by Mary Parish. Reprinted by permission of the author. One line from *Breaking the Glass Ceiling, Updated Edition* (p. 161), copyright © 1992 by Ann M. Morrison, Randall P. White and Ellen Van Velsor. Reprinted by permission of Addison-Wesley Publishing Company, Inc.. One line from *Wishcraft* by Barbara Sher and Anne Gottlieb. Copyright © 1979 by Barbara Sher. Used by permission of Viking Penguin, a division of Penguin Books USA Inc.. One line from *Women in Power* copyright © 1992 by Dorothy W. Cantor and Toni Bernay. Reprinted by permission of Houghton Mifflin Co. All Rights Reserved. One line from *Writing for your Life* by Deena Metzger. Copyright © 1992 by Deena Metzger. Used by permission of HarperCollins Publishers Inc.. Excerpt from 1985 commencement address to Wellesley graduates by Geraldine A. Ferraro. Reprinted by permission of the author. Excerpt from 1984 commencement address to Mt. Holyoke graduates by Barbara B. Kennelly. Reprinted by permission of the author. Excerpt from speech given at 1994 Women of Distinction Awards Dinner by Sheila E. Widnall. Reprinted by permission of the author. Excerpt from 1990 commencement address to Barnard graduates by Madeleine M. Kunin. Reprinted by permission of the author. Excerpt from 1990 commencement address to Smith graduates by Helen Caldicott. Reprinted by permission of the author. Excerpt from speech given by Olympia Dukakis. Reprinted by permission of the author. Excerpt from 1985

about the author

Helene Lerner-Robbins is president of Creative Expansions, Inc. and Oasis Communications. She leads seminars on self-mastery and power, balancing career and family issues, creating mentoring and networking partnerships, and reducing stress for a variety of Fortune 500 corporations, including, Nabisco, Inc., Johnson & Johnson, and Time Warner, Inc. The producer and host of popular television programs on wellness and empowerment topics, she has interviewed hundreds of women. One of her most-watched shows was nominated for an Emmy Award.

A former columnist for *New Woman* magazine, Ms. Lerner-Robbins is the author of several books, including *Embrace Change, Finding Balance,* and *Stress Breakers.* In addition, she maintains a private practice coaching individuals and groups on tools and techniques to increase power in both their personal and professional lives.

A member of Phi Beta Kappa, she holds a Masters degree in Education and an MBA in Management Sciences. She lives in New York City.

She is available for consultation and workshops; for information regarding these programs, contact her in care of Conari Press, 2550 Ninth Street, Suite 101, Berkeley, CA 94710.

Conari Press, established in 1987, publishes books on topics ranging from spirituality and women's history to sexuality and personal growth. Our main goal is to publish quality books that will make a difference in people's lives—both how we feel about ourselves and how we relate to one another.

Our readers are our most important resource, and we value your input, suggestions, and ideas. We'd love to hear from you—after all, we are publishing books for you!

For a complete catalog or to get on our mailing list, please contact us at:

CONARI PRESS

2550 Ninth Street, Suite 101, Berkeley, CA 94710
800-685-9595 · FAX 510-649-7190 · E-MAIL conaripub@aol.com